OPENING ACT

Ann Patrick

A KISMET™ Romance

METEOR PUBLISHING CORPORATION
Bensalem, Pennsylvania

KISMET™ is a trademark of Meteor Publishing Corporation

Copyright © 1990 Patricia A. Kay
Cover art copyright © 1990 Les Katz

All rights reserved.

No part of this book may be reproduced, stored in a retrieval system, or transmitted in any form, by any means, including mechanical, electronic, photocopying, recording or otherwise, without prior written permission of the publisher, Meteor Publishing Corporation, 3369 Progress Drive, Bensalem, PA 19020.

First Printing November 1990.

ISBN: 1-878702-16-5

All the characters in this book are fictitious. Any resemblance to actual persons, living or dead, is purely coincidental.

Printed in the United States of America.

For Phyllis Taylor Pianka, who gave me encouragement and praise when I needed it; and Susan Brown, who told me not to change a single word. Special thanks to Alaina Richardson, Betty Gyenes, Joyce Warwick, and Elaine Kimberley, whose support guided me over the rough spots.

ANN PATRICK

Ann Patrick was the kind of kid who always had her nose stuck in a book. For years she dreamed about being a writer. Finally, when her three children were grown, she decided to do something about her lifelong wish and has been writing ever since. "I love writing," she says. "There's no greater thrill in the world than having someone say they like what you've written." Ann and her husband, along with their two cats, live in Houston, Texas.

ONE

Alex Summerfield saw the flashing blue lights before he heard the siren. He swore as he hit the brakes. The powerful Mercedes responded immediately, and Alex pulled to the side of the road as he muttered, "Where the hell did *he* come from?"

The tan car with the revolving dome light pulled up behind him. Alex watched in his rearview mirror as the car door opened and booted feet appeared. "It's your own fault," he said aloud. He hadn't been paying attention to his driving at all; he'd been too preoccupied. Besides, the deserted upstate New York road had lulled him into a false sense of isolation. And now he was going to pay for his daydreaming.

He'd heard about these speed traps. These backwoods cops had a reputation for hiding behind trees and waiting for some unsuspecting city type like him to come along.

Alex leaned over and fished around in his glove compartment until he found his registration. Hearing the crunch of gravel, he turned, pushed the button that controlled his electric window, and looked up.

Staring down at him from under the wide brim of a dark brown Stetson was a young woman with the bluest eyes he'd ever seen.

"Hello . . . uh, officer," Alex said.

Miss Blue-Eyes didn't blink. She also didn't smile. And females of all ages usually smiled when they set eyes on Alex. For a moment Alex felt uncertain, then he thought, so she's a cop. So what? She's also a woman. Smiling brightly, he mustered the considerable Summerfield charm and said, "Was I speeding, officer? Sorry. Guess I was daydreaming. The scenery around here is so beautiful; I forgot all about my driving. Believe me, it won't happen again." Then he chuckled. "And how many times have you heard that one?"

"May I see your driver's license and registration, please."

The words were clipped and brisk. Her expression didn't change, and the blue eyes peering at him from just below the wide brim of her hat studied him intently. Alex frowned. What was *her* problem? PMS? He pulled his wallet from his pocket, opened it, then handed her his driver's license.

"Mr. Summerfield. Do you know how fast you were going?"

"No, officer. I'm afraid I don't." Alex kept his voice conciliatory even though he was tempted to answer sarcastically. He might still be able to charm his way out of this.

The woman officer's face remained impassive, and

her voice lacked any hint of warmth. "I clocked you at 67 miles per hour. Do you know what the speed limit is on this road?"

Alex angrily thumped his fingers on the steering wheel. Good Lord, it wasn't as if he had endangered anyone's life or anything. There wasn't another car on the road. Not a soul had gone by since she'd pulled him over. Didn't she have anything better to do than hassle him? "Yes, I do," he said. "I saw a sign a couple of miles back. It's 35, isn't it?" He forced himself to keep his answer polite.

"Yes. It's 35. And for good reason. This road, even though it looks deserted, is used by many of the farmers in the area. If you'd come around a curve going as fast as you were going and a slow-moving vehicle was ahead of you—say a tractor or a combine —you'd have run right into it. Driving that fast is irresponsible and dangerous. You should know better."

Tired from long hours of driving and accustomed to the combative atmosphere of New York City's streets, Alex forgot all about charming her. "Oh, come on, lady. Give me a break. I explained what happened. I was thinking about something else, and I didn't realize how fast I was going. It's not that big a deal, so if you're going to give me a ticket, just give it to me, and save the lectures."

Now the blue eyes came alive. They flashed as bright as the dome light on her car. "When you speak to me, Mr. Summerfield, the proper form of address is 'Officer,' not 'Lady.' And breaking the law and endangering the lives of innocent people *is* a big deal. This isn't New York City. This is Juliette where we care about people, where everyone is treated the same way, where it doesn't matter *who* you are when it comes to the laws." She opened her pad, whipped out a pen, clicked it open with a gesture that could only be classified as smug, and began writing.

So she did know who he was. In fact, Alex wouldn't be at all surprised if she was making a big thing out of this for that very reason. He knew he should just keep his mouth shut, take the ticket, and chalk the whole episode up to experience. But there was something about the way Miss Smarty-Pants had curled her lip as she delivered her last salvo that caused him to shove caution out the door.

"Well, *officer*," he drawled, "in New York City the cops are too busy dealing with real crime to worry much about someone driving a little too fast. Of course, up here you don't have that much to do. I realize that. So why don't you just write the damned citation and go home and dust off your bullets."

Her eyes narrowed, and her nostrils flared. He almost smiled—he'd obviously hit on a sore spot—but a last remnant of good sense overrode the ill-advised urge. Two pink spots appeared on her cheeks, and the blue eyes were fired with angry light.

"For your information, *Mr*. Summerfield, I happen to consider any law important, and any crime real crime. And if you don't *like* the way we do things here, you can turn your car around and go back the way you came." She thrust the pad under his nose. "Sign it!"

Alex signed it. The paper crackled as he handed

the pad back, and for a moment he met her blazing eyes. Cobalt blue. They sure were pretty; she sure was cute. But she was also madder than a wasp trapped between a screen and a window. Her full lips were set in a straight, uncompromising line, and the thought popped into Alex's mind that those lips were just the right shape for kissing. He itched to say so. He wondered what she'd do if he smiled at her and said, "What are you so mad about? A girl as pretty as you shouldn't be out here playing at cop. She should be at home warming someone's bed and having the socks kissed off her."

Something of what he was thinking must have shown in his eyes, because she took a deep breath, causing her chest to rise and pull the khaki material of her shirt tightly across her rounded breasts. For the first time, Alex noticed the name sewn across the top of her breast pocket. VALETTI.

"Goodbye, Mr. Summerfield," she said. "Instructions on how to pay your fine are printed on the back of that ticket." Then an evil smile curved her lips. "Of course, you may think you're so far above the law you don't have to pay tickets. Maybe you're one of those city types who tear them up and throw them away." Her tone and the expression in her eyes said, "I dare you to ignore the ticket."

Alex opened his mouth to retort in kind, but his good sense finally reasserted itself. Closing his mouth, he watched her walk back to her car. The uniform hugged her body tightly, revealing every shapely curve. Too bad she was so up-tight. Alex wondered how she'd look without that hat. He'd only caught a glimpse of her hair, but what he could see of it that wasn't tucked up under the Stetson had looked heavy and rich and dark and shining—the kind of hair a man would love to get his hands into. Everything about her suggested the kind of girl who belonged in a filmy pink dress and picture hat—not the kind of girl to have a gun strapped to her hip and to be wearing a man's pants and boots.

She looked exactly like the kind of girl he'd like to get to know better. Cute and feisty. Totally unsophisticated and opposite to the brittle and glamorous women he'd spent the last ten years around. Then he grinned. Fat chance of that. That little deputy sheriff or whatever she was would probably spit on him if she ever saw him again. Besides, since Margo had left, he'd sworn off women. All they were was trouble. And Alex didn't need trouble. What he did need was peace. Peace, quiet, and a place to work. Which was just what he had ahead of him—a long, quiet summer to get his career back in gear.

Alex started his car, darted one more glance in his rearview mirror, then carefully pulled onto the road and sedately pushed his speed to 35 and kept it there.

For the rest of the morning and on into the afternoon, Sheriff Veronica Valetti tried to put her encounter with Broadway Big Mouth out of her mind. But at odd moments, she'd find herself remembering his amused, insolent attitude, and she'd get furious all over again.

Wasn't it just typical? she thought. The moment Alexander Summerfield had realized she was a woman he hadn't been prepared to take her seriously. If she'd been a man, he'd never have said the kinds of things he'd said to her.

Ronnie was sick of that superior male attitude. She'd had enough of it from the men in Juliette County, and now here came this big shot playwright —oh, she knew who he was all right, even though she hadn't let on to him—and instead of being enlightened, as Ronnie would have expected him to be, he was just as bad—no, *worse*—than the men who'd watched her grow up.

Well, she thought, as she gritted her teeth and dug into a pile of paperwork, the men around here had come to respect her. Even the ones who thought she'd only gotten her position as a deputy sheriff because her father had appointed her before his death had had to change their tune when she was elected sheriff last November. Since then she'd made great inroads in cleaning up the county, shown people what an efficient, honest organization was like. She had a lot to be proud of. She smiled. Her father would have been very proud of her, too.

Still smiling, she picked up a report waiting for her signature. A few minutes later, the door to her office opened and her cousin, Sam Barzini, burst in. His pudgy face was the exact shade of ripe strawberries. "You gotta come right now, Ronnie," he shouted. "It's an emergency!"

"Calm down, Sam," she said as she swung her legs off her desk. "What's the problem?"

"Hector! He's got Hector, and he won't give him back to me!"

Trying to keep a straight face, Ronnie said, "Who's got Hector?" What she really meant was, who'd want Hector?

"Our new tenant. The one who moved in today." Sam huffed and swiped at his forehead dotted with sweat beads like those plastic bubbles in wrapping material. He drew a raggedy breath. "Please, Ronnie. Don't just stand there. This is serious. He's threatening to drown Hector."

It was Ronnie's personal opinion that if someone *did* drown Hector, the world would be an infinitely better place to live, but she knew how much Sam loved his ornery cat, so she sighed and said, "Okay. Okay. I'm coming." She'd been so annoyed by her encounter with that neanderthal Summerfield this morning, she'd forgotten all about Bernie Maxwell, the man who'd rented Sam's carriage house for the summer. She and Sam had both been curious about Maxwell. He knew about the house through a friend who'd stayed there years ago, and the complete transaction had been done by phone and mail. All Sam knew about him was that he was a theatrical agent.

"I'll be back soon," she called to Maisie, the dispatcher for the day shift. "Got a little problem up at the house."

Maisie gave Ronnie thumbs up to show she understood, and Ronnie followed Sam out the front door. She sprinted to keep up with him as he scurried ahead like a frightened rabbit. Ronnie had never seen her forty-year-old cousin move so fast. She hadn't known he *could* move that fast. Sam wasn't exactly the outdoor, love-to-exercise, eat-healthy-food type.

In fact, Ronnie had been after him for years to change his eating habits, but so far all he'd done was ignore her.

Five minutes later, after traversing the three quarters of a mile to the house she shared with Sam, Ronnie felt slightly winded. Time to start jogging again, she thought. She'd been slacking off lately, and what if someone robbed the Juliette Savings and Loan and the perpetrator tried to escape on foot? As the chief law enforcement officer in Juliette County, she'd be required to give hot pursuit. Ronnie rested a hand over her thumping heart. And she'd be in big trouble.

Sam didn't stop when they reached the house; he just kept going on down the gravel driveway to the back of the property and the old carriage house. He took great gulps of air; then in a wheezing breath he said, "I knew as soon as I saw him I wasn't gonna like him. Thinks he's hot stuff."

Thinks he's hot stuff. Sam's assessment of Bernie Maxwell reminded Ronnie of her encounter with Alexander Summerfield this morning. Alexander Summerfield. She still couldn't believe it. Even in Juliette, a place he obviously considered a backwater county, Ronnie was aware of Summerfield's accomplishments. Ronnie loved the theater, and before her father died she would go down to the city with him several times a year to see the new Broadway plays. But now, what with the demands of her new job, she hadn't been able to take much time off for fun.

But even so, she knew of Alexander Summerfield, acclaimed playwright and a bona fide boy wonder, with one hit play after another. She couldn't help but know him. She also couldn't help but wish she'd met him under different circumstances, even though it had been disappointing to discover he was a smart ass who thought he could charm his way out of anything. It had been obvious to her that he thought he was better than the people of Juliette.

" . . . and he said *I hate cats.*"

Guiltily, Ronnie jerked herself back to Sam and the present situation. "I'm sorry, Sam. What did you say?"

"I said, I asked him if I could help him with his things, and Hector was there with me. You know how he follows me everywhere. And he took one look at Hector and said *I hate cats.*" With his furrowed brow and wide brown eyes, Sam's face was a picture of indignation as he took one labored breath after another.

Ronnie worried about Sam. He was much too fat, and all this excitement couldn't be good for him. Patting him on the arm, she smothered a smile. As a rule, Ronnie liked cats, but she hated Hector. Most people hated Hector. Actually, most *cats* hated Hector, not to mention dogs, birds, and insects. Hector was a big, fat, pain in the butt. His favorite pastime was crouching down under the bushes in front of the house while waiting for some unsuspecting soul to walk past. Then he would pounce, sinking his sharp teeth into his victim's ankle or calf. Ronnie had been the object of this form of torture several times. She would have drowned Hector herself years ago except that she loved Sam. Besides her brothers, he was the only family she had left. When her father died, Sam had never let her feel alone.

Besides, she'd never been able to catch Hector.

Making clucking sounds to reassure Sam, Ronnie thought fast. "So the new tenant *caught* Hector?"

"I know it's hard to believe. I don't know how he did it. All I know is, I'd gone back in the house, and about twenty minutes later I called Hector to come and eat." Sam's dark eyes were filled with worry. "You know how much Hector likes to eat."

That's an understatement, she thought. Next to attacking innocent people, Hector liked nothing better than stuffing his chops. If a person wasn't careful, he'd snatch food right from under your nose. To protect food from Hector meant guarding it like the crown jewels.

"Anyway," Sam continued, "I called and called, but Hector wouldn't come, so I went outside and started looking around, all the while calling his name. Then that . . . that idiot walked outside and said, cool as a cucumber, '*Looking for your cat? Don't bother. He's locked up in my broom closet.*' "

Ronnie pressed her lips together. She wanted to laugh so badly she didn't know where to look, but Sam's eyebrows were pinched together and his voice was full of agony as he cried, "Ronnie, he was serious! He said he was going to drown Hector, and he walked back into the carriage house. He wouldn't listen to me!" Sam wrung his hands together. "What should we do?"

Ronnie sighed again and wished she could turn

around, walk away and leave Hector to his well-deserved fate, but Sam was depending on her. "Don't worry," she said. "I'll take care of it." She took a deep breath, squared her shoulders and lifted the brass knocker on the carriage house door, banging it down three or four times.

When the door opened, Ronnie almost toppled over from shock. She couldn't believe her eyes. Her mouth fell open, and she stared. Alexander Summerfield stared back. Part of her registered the fact that he really was drop-dead gorgeous; she hadn't been wrong in her first impression of him. And now that she could see all of him, he was even better looking than she'd first thought, with thick black hair threaded with silver and eyes that reminded her of gray cashmere. What was *he* doing in the carriage house? Where was Bernie Maxwell?

"Well, well, well. What have we here?" Alexander Summerfield said. "I do believe it's the same law-enforcement officer I had the pleasure of meeting earlier today. Still hot on the heels of criminals, officer? What law have I broken now?" His gray eyes glittered like smoky diamonds, and the hint of a smile lurked around his well-shaped mouth.

He stood with his hands on his hips. His toasty brown skin and the smooth muscles of his arms and chest were clearly visible in the scanty covering of a gray T-shirt. He wore black nylon running shorts, and on his feet were a beat-up pair of Nikes. Sweat glistened on his exposed skin.

Ronnie realized she was gawking. She gave herself a mental shake. So he was gorgeous. So what? Just because there were no gorgeous men in Juliette, except for Ed Traymore, who owned the hardware store and didn't count because he was married and had five kids—soon to be six—was no excuse for her to act like a stage-door groupie.

"Uh . . ." she said, then could have bitten her tongue off. That's great, Valetti, she told herself. Just great. Stand there and stare for ten minutes, then say *uh*. That's real professional. That's the way to show your authority and competence.

Forcing herself to quit looking at his body, Ronnie cleared her throat, drew herself up to her full five-feet-two and said firmly, "Hello, Mr. Summerfield." *I will not lose my temper*.

"You have me at a disadvantage, officer. You know my name, but I don't know yours." Now there was more than a hint of a smile on his face. The gray eyes were filled with mocking amusement as they dropped to the vicinity of her chest.

Ronnie debated whether to smack the smirk off his face or ignore his attempt to goad her into a childish retort. She knew darn well he had read her name on her breast pocket. Her good sense won out, and she replied evenly, "I'm Sheriff Valetti, Mr. Summerfield, and Sam . . . Mr. Barzini . . ." She gestured in Sam's direction. ". . . has informed me that you have captured his pet cat and refuse to release him. Is that correct?"

Alexander Summerfield's gray eyes continued to study her with a lazy warmth, and Ronnie's heart did crazy leap-frog type things. His smile expanded into a grin, and perfect white teeth sparkled like new-fallen snow. "Yes, that's correct," he said in the husky, low voice she'd noticed earlier. "But I meant your *first* name."

His voice shimmered over her body. "My first name is irrelevant," she said, trying to keep her mind on the subject at hand and ignore his blatant sex appeal. "And it's against the law to steal someone's pet." Don't be swayed by his smile, she told herself. Remember, he thinks he's God's gift to women.

The smile disappeared but not completely. There was still a hint of laughter in his eyes as he looked at her, looked her up and down in a way that made her squirm uneasily. She wondered what he was thinking. Then she wasn't sure she really wanted to know. It would probably make her mad.

"I should also think it's against the law for someone's *pet* to leap out at someone and attempt to tear them apart." He turned around and pointed to his well-formed calf muscle—now blemished by distinct puncture wounds. "I thought you told me that all laws are important to you. If I remember your exact words you said everyone is treated the same here, no matter who the person is. But now it looks as if the laws are different for the people who live here and the people who visit here."

Ronnie winced at his words. He was right. And Sam was in the wrong. It really didn't matter that Hector had had his shots and that he'd never really hurt anyone when he'd gone into his tiger act before. Hector was a nuisance, and his bites hurt.

"The laws *do* apply equally to everyone, Mr.

Summerfield. Hector shouldn't be permitted to attack people, but it isn't up to you to decide on punishment or keep him imprisoned. He's not your property. Now, show me where he is, and I'll take care of this."

Ignoring her order, Alexander Summerfield said, "I don't know why any sane person would want a cat like that." He raised his eyebrows, and the left one went up higher than the right.

Fascinated, Ronnie watched it quiver there. "I realize Hector is a little aggressive at times—"

"A little aggressive? That's hardly an apt description. I'd have selected words like vicious and predatory and a public menace."

"Oh, come on, Mr. Summerfield. We're talking about a house cat, not a mountain lion." Although she agreed with him, she had no intention of letting him think he had the upper hand. She'd grown up in a house full of males; she'd learned to deal with male intimidation early in life. She didn't flinch as he stared at her, the amusement in his eyes returning. I refuse to smile, she thought. He's entirely too sure of himself. His charm didn't work before, and it won't work now.

"Easy for you to say," he countered. "You're not the one standing here with bite marks on *your* leg. For all I know, I could get rabies. That orange hellcat belongs in the jungle."

"You won't get rabies, if that's what you're so worried about," Sam said. "Hector's had all his shots. I'll show you the papers."

The two men glared at each other, and Ronnie

sighed. Males could be so childish. "Mr. Summerfield. Let's try to be reasonable, shall we? It's ridiculous for us to stand here arguing. Do you, or do you not, intend to release Sam's cat?"

"I do not." His eyes now glinted like shining steel.

"I see." Good grief, what now? It wasn't as if she were facing a bank robber or a rapist or even a murderer. She'd been in the right earlier today, but this episode was a different story. She'd feel a bit silly pulling out her gun and threatening him.

"Now, see here," Sam sputtered. "You'd better give Hector back to me, or Ronnie . . . Sheriff Valetti . . . will just have to arrest you."

Ronnie cringed, but she loyally backed up Sam's threat. "He's right, Mr. Summerfield. If you refuse to release the cat peacefully, I'll have to invoke the law." Although uneasy about the look in Alexander Summerfield's eyes, she refused to drop her gaze. Instead she returned his glittering stare unflinchingly. Her insides felt like a twisted pretzel, and she could feel her face heat under his scrutiny.

The silence stretched. The only sounds were the chirping of robins and the buzzing of bees around the lilac bushes and the hum of a motor bike on the road beyond.

Finally Alexander Summerfield spoke. "I'll let you come in and get the cat on one condition."

Ronnie bristled at the term *condition*, but she said, "And that is?" Right now all she wanted was the return of Hector, so that Sam would calm down. She'd deal with Mr. Perfection later.

"That Barzini keep his cat confined. I do not intend to run the risk of being bitten by that fleabag every time I set foot out of my front door."

"But—" Sam protested.

"Or," Alexander Summerfield continued, staring at Sam, "if you prefer, I'll go out and buy myself a nice, big, cat-eating Doberman!"

"Now just a cotton-pickin' minute!" Sam exclaimed. "I'm getting a little fed up with you!"

Ronnie glared at Sam. *Be quiet*, the look said. She turned to Summerfield. "We agree to your condition."

"Good. I knew you'd see it my way." He moved aside in the doorway. "You can come in and get the cat."

Ronnie nudged a still-sputtering Sam past Alexander Summerfield before he could change his mind. They found Hector, none the worse for his confinement, but fighting mad, skulking in the back of the broom closet in the kitchen.

"It's okay, Hector," Sam crooned as he petted the loudly complaining cat. "You're all right."

Hector spied his tormentor and bared his teeth, hissing and spitting in fury.

"Thank you, Mr. Summerfield," Ronnie murmured as she took Sam's arm. "Let's go," she muttered, "before your mountain lion here decides to strike again." Hector's coppery fur stood straight up as they made their escape.

Ronnie looked back once on her way out. Alexander Summerfield leaned against the door frame of the open kitchen doorway, and for a long moment, their eyes locked. Then he very slowly gave her a once-over, letting his silvery eyes glide down her body, then back up. The corners of his wide mouth quirked up.

A queer breathlessness seized Ronnie. What was he looking at? She nearly voiced the question, then thought better of it. Just ignore him, she told herself. He wants you to lose your temper and say something stupid. Don't do it.

"I wonder what great crime will bring us together next time, sheriff," he drawled.

Don't answer.

"Maybe I'll be playing my stereo too loud . . ."

Don't answer.

"Or maybe it'll be something really serious like whistling at pretty girls on Main Street . . ."

Ronnie whirled around. "Listen, Big Shot, don't try to impress me with how witty you are because you're wasting your breath. Most of the time . . ." She paused for emphasis. "Most of the time I'm called out about serious problems, not because someone is making a nuisance of himself!"

"No kidding?" His eyes twinkled. "The men in your department stand for that?"

Ronnie knew she should have left five minutes ago. "What's that remark supposed to mean?"

With that infuriating twinkle still in his eyes, he said slowly, deliberately, "I figured you for the catnapping, ticket writing detail, and the men for the serious crime detail. You know—the kinds of problems a female half-pint like you can't handle."

Ronnie's temper exploded. She wanted to kick

him. Instead she settled for putting her hands on her hips and glaring at him. "Listen, you Neanderthal," she said, "I'm almost thirty years old, I've got a degree in law enforcement and criminal justice, I've been with the sheriff's department for nearly seven years, and I can handle anything that comes my way. And that includes you!"

TWO

He laughed out loud. "Thirty years old. Who'd have believed it?"

"What's that supposed to mean?"

He shrugged, the infuriating smirk still plastered to his face. "Just that I'd have pegged you for about eighteen."

Eighteen! Looking young was the bane of Ronnie's existence, but no one had made disparaging remarks about her age for so long, she'd almost forgotten the feeling of impotence and frustration such remarks inspired.

"I may look young," she said with dignity, "but at least *I* act my age, which is more than I can say for you." Then she swung around and marched away, keeping her head high.

"I'm looking forward to our next encounter, sheriff," he called, laughter tinging his words. "Maybe Juliette won't be boring after all."

She refused to give him the satisfaction of answering him, no matter how much she wanted to. She muttered all the way back to her office. She hadn't acquitted herself well this afternoon, despite what she'd said to Mr. Know-it-all. And it was no consolation that he would probably be quite embarrassed when he discovered she lived not twenty feet from his back door, and that they were going to be neighbors for the entire summer. Just because he'd made fun of her was no reason for her to lose control and lash back at him. She was an officer of the law, for God's sake. She should have been cool, calm, professional. That was the only way to put men like Alexander Summerfield in their place.

She sighed heavily, but since there wasn't anyone in her office, the sigh was wasted as high drama. Damn. It had been a frustrating day. She'd admired Alexander Summerfield's work for years, and now he'd turned out to be a conceited smart-mouth. And to top it all off, he'd managed to make her lose her temper, which had brought her down to his level.

But no matter how many times she told herself he was a jerk, not worth paying any attention to, it rankled to know he thought she was someone to joke about, someone not to be taken seriously. Oh, what difference did it make what he thought of her? Alexander Summerfield was obviously pompous and arrogant. In fact, she couldn't stand him. He represented the very worst in male egocentricity, and he could go stuff himself.

Trying to forget the unfortunate set of circumstances surrounding her two meetings with her new neighbor, Ronnie wandered back to the bathroom and looked at herself in the mirror. She took the pins out of her hair, brushed it, then twisted it back up and repinned it. Fiddle. No matter what she did, she looked the same. Young. If only she were taller. One time when she'd had to appear in court she met a lawyer named Jeanne something, who was tall and elegant, with straight blonde hair, a precise, deep voice, and an angular figure that looked wonderful in tailored clothes. She had commanded respect not only because she was smart and competent but because she looked the part of a professional with her grown-up face.

Ronnie hated her own face. It was too round, too little-girl looking. She hated it when people did a double-take when they found out she was almost thirty years old. She knew that in today's world she was probably in the minority. Most women were obsessed with looking young and would give anything to be taken for ten years younger than they actually were. But most women hadn't been fighting for respect in a profession where how you looked might make the difference in how a criminal reacted to you. Or whether the voters voted for you.

And, Ronnie admitted to herself, most women hadn't just come up against the ridicule of Alexander Summerfield. The same Alexander Summerfield who had written *A Day for Lovers* and *Good Neighbors* and *Big Girls Don't Cry* and *Weeping Willow*. Plays that had made Ronnie laugh and cry. Plays that were gripping and sensitive and emotion-packed.

That's what puzzled her about him. How could he write plays with the kind of depth his contained?

There *must* be more to him than good looks and arrogance.

Her pride demanded that he respect her, that he think of her as a capable, intelligent woman. Someone interesting.

Someone he might be interested in.

Ronnie felt her face heat as the unbidden thought crept insidiously into her mind. Come on, Valetti, she lectured herself. You're not *really* attracted to him, are you? No, of course not. She only wanted him to be interested in her so she could spurn him. After all, she rationalized, it would give her the greatest pleasure to knock him down a peg or two. Show him there were women in the world immune to his sex appeal.

Grinning, Ronnie went back to her office and attacked the stack of paperwork she'd abandoned earlier. But throughout the afternoon her mind kept wandering back to the carriage house and the sound of Alexander Summerfield's throaty laugh as she'd made her ignominious retreat.

When Miss Prissy-Pants and his rotund landlord disappeared from Alex Summerfield's view, he was still chuckling. What had possessed him to bait the little sheriff like that? He hadn't behaved this badly toward anyone in years, and he couldn't imagine why he'd done it today.

But the sight of her, so furious, with those enormous blue eyes and that shiny mass of chestnut-colored hair, had been irresistible. She'd been so mad. Her creamy cheeks had flushed an attractive shade of pink, and the smattering of golden freckles decorating her tip-tilted nose had deepened to pale amber.

Golden freckles? Tip-tilted nose? Alex gave himself a mental shake. Thinking like that was dangerous. He had more important things to do with his time than daydream about a woman. *Remember Margo.* Thinking of his ex-wife caused Alex's lighthearted mood to darken. Getting involved with a demanding woman was what had put him in this fix to start with. He'd better remember that. So no matter how intriguing the pretty sheriff was—Ronnie, that was what Barzini had called her—no matter how tempting it might be to find out more about her, he'd better put her out of his mind. He'd better remember he'd sworn off women—and why.

Determinedly, Alex turned and walked into the sunny kitchen. Opening the refrigerator, he removed a bottle of Beck's beer from the supply he'd stocked earlier. As the cool, rich brew slid down his throat, he closed his eyes.

Okay, Summerfield, he told himself. You're here to get *Signposts* whipped into shape. Remember that. You can't afford any involvements or distractions. It's been three years since you've written anything worth two cents. Your involvement, no, your *obsession* with Margo was the reason you couldn't write anything. Remember that. Keep your mind on your goal, and forget all about women.

Besides, Bernie would kill him if he screwed up again. Alex smiled as he thought of Bernie. Bernie Maxwell: his agent, friend, and father confessor. He was the one who had recommended the drastic change in Alex's lifestyle and the one who had arranged for the rental of the carriage house for the summer.

"Richard Girard, an old friend of mine, stayed there one summer, and I went up to visit him," Bernie said. "I was really taken with the place. It's perfect for your purposes—pretty, quiet, and the people are great. You should get a lot of work done."

Alex walked slowly over to the open window and stared out. Lush maple, elm, and silver birch trees shaded the yard, as well as a half dozen fruit trees. Colorful beds of flowers decorated the property. The view was radically different than the view from his New York apartment. Alex hoped Bernie was right and this tiny hamlet would prove to be the sanctuary he needed.

Turning away from the window, Alex decided to call Bernie, then finish unpacking and take a walk to explore the town. He picked up the phone and pressed the familiar numbers.

"Hey, kid. How's it goin'?" Bernie's voice boomed across the long-distance wire. "Settled in all right?"

"Yes. You were right, Bernie. Juliette's a beautiful place, and I think the peace and quiet are exactly what I need right now."

"I know I'm right, kid. Mark my words, stayin' away from the bright lights and the foxes will be just the ticket. You'll get that play whipped into shape in no time."

"I hope so," Alex said. "When do you plan to come up?"

"Sometime toward the end of July. And I expect

you to have Act II and most of Act III revised and polished by then."

Alex sighed. "I'll try, Bern."

"Don't try. Just do it."

When Ronnie arrived home that evening, she pulled into the parking area behind the house. Sam's beat-up Chevy pickup truck was parked in its usual spot and next to it, gleaming with wax, rested Alexander Summerfield's silver Mercedes. Probably bought it to match his eyes, Ronnie thought maliciously.

As she climbed the outside steps to her second floor apartment, she glanced back at the carriage house. All the windows were open; filmy white curtains billowed out in the afternoon breeze.

It was a glorious day—clear and sunny. Ronnie decided she really did need to get some exercise. After letting herself in, she walked through her apartment and opened all the windows. Then she poured herself a cold glass of lemonade; she slowly sipped it and glanced through her mail.

A bill from the electric company. An envelope containing an offer to go look at some land around Lake George. And a letter from Kate.

Ronnie grinned. Kate Chamberlin had been her college roommate and had remained her best friend ever since. Kate lived in New York City and worked for a big advertising agency which meant she and Ronnie didn't get to see each other as often as they'd like, but they were faithful about calling and writing.

Settling down to read Kate's letter, Ronnie chuckled at Kate's latest anecdotes about dating in the city.

Kate's contention was that there were no good men in New York City. "They're either gay or married or divorced and have no intention of marrying again," she'd complained just a few weeks ago.

"Well, there are no men at all in Juliette," Ronnie had answered, "so I don't feel sorry for you."

"Come on, Ronnie," Kate said. "What about William?" Then they both laughed.

William was one of Ronnie's deputies. He was only twenty-one years old, but that hadn't stopped him from trying to jump her bones every chance he got. Ronnie's theory about William was that he thought it manly to put the move on her whether he was interested or not. She could just see the wheels turning in his head. Older woman. Probably experienced. Mark another notch on the old belt.

After finishing Kate's letter, Ronnie put on her running shoes and blue shorts and a white T-shirt and walked outside.

Keeping an eye on the door of the carriage house, she slowly did stretching exercises on the porch, but she saw no sign of her new neighbor. Straightening, she ran lightly down the steps; then, gathering speed, she jogged down the walk, gaining momentum with each stride. Reaching the corner of the house, she made a sharp left turn and ran smack into a rock-solid wall of flesh.

"Look out!"

Strong hands gripped her shoulders.

Heart hammering and head spinning from the impact of her collision with him, Ronnie looked up, cursing herself for her carelessness.

Alexander Summerfield grinned down at her. "Were you looking for me?" he said.

His warm, smooth palms slid down her bare arms. Ronnie's insides bounced around like Mexican jumping beans. If she'd thought he looked gorgeous before, she couldn't think what adjective to apply to him now. He looked as if he'd just stepped out of the shower. His dark hair glistened as the late afternoon sun shimmered on its surface. Dressed in a pair of pale gray cotton pants and a white cotton shirt open at the throat, he smelled like sandalwood and looked like every girl's summertime dream.

"Don't flatter yourself," she said.

He grinned: that disarming grin that had so infuriated her earlier. The grin seemed to say he knew exactly what she'd been thinking, despite her words to the contrary.

"Well, if you're not looking for me, what *are* you doing here?"

"I live here."

"Live here? I thought Barzini lived here."

"He does." She was tempted to smile as she saw the confusion that flitted across his face.

"I see," he said slowly. The teasing twinkle in his eyes faded, replaced with knowing disdain.

"No, you don't see," Ronnie said, although why she felt compelled to explain to him, she didn't know. "Sam is my cousin. He lives downstairs. I live in the upstairs apartment."

Now the knowing look disappeared, and Alexander Summerfield had the grace to look embarrassed.

Then, with that hint of arrogance and hidden amusement she detested, he drawled, "So we're neighbors."

"Yes. Now, if you don't mind, you'll have to excuse me. I was just starting to run." She turned away. "Goodbye, Mr. Summerfield."

His hand stopped her as it closed around her upper arm. He gently turned her around to face him again. "Hey," he said softly, "don't go away mad."

Ronnie took a deep breath. "I'm not mad, Mr. Summerfield. I'm just not interested in continuing this conversation."

"I'm sorry we got off to such a bad start. Since we're neighbors, it would be nice if we could be friends."

That'll never happen, Ronnie thought. He was much too sure of himself: too conceited, too arrogant, too handsome, and most of all—too unsettling—for them to be friends. She shrugged.

Obviously taking her shrug for agreement, he smiled. "Now that we've settled that, how about calling me Alex instead of Mr. Summerfield? Mr. Summerfield makes me feel like an old man." He chuckled, running his fingers through his hair. "And despite these gray hairs that you see, I'm only thirty-seven."

"I—" Oh, what the heck, she thought. It would take more energy to stay mad at him than it would to go along with him. And he *was* living awfully close. "Sure . . . Alex," she said.

"And what do I call you? Sheriff?" His eyes twinkled.

"My name is Veronica, but everyone calls me Ronnie."

"Veronica," he repeated softly. "A lovely name. Unusual, too." His eyes were filled with warmth as they rested on her face.

For just a moment, Ronnie felt totally unnerved by his gaze. Then she shook off the feeling. "Veronica was my grandmother's name." Now why had she told him that?

"Why don't you use it? Why do people call you Ronnie?"

"My mother died with I was just a baby, and I guess Dad wasn't sure what to do with a girl. He's the one who called me Ronnie, and the name stuck."

"I like Veronica much better. May I call you Veronica?"

The way he said her name, rolling it on his tongue, caused her heart to accelerate. Damn the man. Why did he make her feel like a star-struck teenager? "Mr. Summerfield—"

"Alex."

"Alex." Ronnie wet her lips and watched his eyes follow her tongue. She could feel herself flushing. Oh, it was infuriating that she couldn't control her emotions around him. That lawyer, the one named Jeanne, would have probably cut him down to size with several well-chosen words, whereas Ronnie couldn't think of anything to say that wouldn't make her sound petty. "Call me whatever you like," she finally said. "It's entirely up to you." She didn't intend to see him often enough that it would matter. She intended to avoid him if at all possible. She didn't like the feelings he evoked in her. Ronnie liked being in control, and from the moment she'd set eyes on him, she'd felt herself whirling *out* of control.

"Good. Now, why don't you go have your run, and then when you're finished, why don't you let me take you out for a hamburger or something? We can get to know each other better."

"Mr. Summerfield—"

"Alex."

Ronnie sighed heavily. "Alex, what makes you think I want to get to know you better?"

His silvery eyes gleamed with amusement. "Just what is it about me that you dislike so much?"

"Everything," she said before she could stop herself.

"Everything?" His lips quivered. "That's going to make it tough. Everything, huh?"

Ronnie studied the toe of her left shoe. This whole conversation was ridiculous. Why hadn't she just terminated it and run off? Now she felt stupid and silly. A definite disadvantage around the sophisticated Alex Summerfield.

"Well, I like everything about you," he drawled.

Ronnie's stomach curled up, and her breathing quickened. Slowly, she raised her head, and their eyes met. She knew her cheeks were pink.

"And I'm not holding it against you that you nearly arrested me twice today," he added, voice low and teasing.

"I was just doing my job," Ronnie said automatically, but her heart wasn't in it, and she knew he knew it.

"It's still hard for me to believe that a tiny female

like you is sheriff. You don't look big enough or strong enough for a job like that."

All her life Ronnie had fought against the misconceptions her size caused. Her father and her brothers had both tried to discourage her from pursuing a career in law enforcement, even after she'd successfully received a degree in criminal justice and law enforcement. Her father had grudgingly appointed her a deputy sheriff, warning her that she'd have to work twice as hard as anyone else because of who she was as well as because of her sex and appearance.

She'd proven she could handle the job, though, and before her father died five years ago, he'd admitted as much.

"You've done a great job, Ronnie. I'm proud of you."

Her heart had swelled with happiness at this accolade from the father she'd always adored. His respect meant more than anything else. It was then that she'd vowed to run for sheriff herself some day—to show everyone that she was her father's daughter—that she could do anything she put her mind to.

"You know, Alex," she said now, "it's pretty hard for me to believe you're the serious writer you're reputed to be, too. In my experience, pretty boys usually don't have much upstairs." Ronnie punctuated her words with stabbing motions to her head.

He threw back his head and laughed. "Touché," he said. "I guess I deserved that."

"Yes, you did. Now please excuse me. I really do have to get my run in."

"What about the hamburger later?"

"I don't think so," she said politely. "But thank you for asking." She gave him a mock salute and jogged up the driveway. She could feel his eyes on her, and she had a childish urge to turn around and stick her tongue out at him.

"Hey," he called. "You're missing a great opportunity to educate me. Wouldn't you like to prove me wrong in all my assumptions about you?"

Ronnie stopped. Ignore him, her inner voice said. He means nothing but trouble. She heard the crunch of gravel as he walked toward her. She turned around slowly.

They were standing at the edge of the driveway, where it met the road. Suddenly she was acutely aware of every sight and sound around her. Wild violets sprouted along the road in deep purple clumps. She could hear Sam's T.V. set blaring away inside the house and the muffled clink of dishes from the O'Hara house next door as well as the happy shouts of children at play. The tantalizing aroma of a neighbor's barbecue floated in the warm air. The sun's deep golden rays slanted across Alex's tanned, square face, and his eyes sparkled as they rested on her face.

"Come on," he said. "Let's call a truce." He stuck out his hand.

Against her better judgment, Ronnie extended her hand. As his warm hand enfolded hers, her breathing quickened. There was something about the way he was looking at her that made her go all soft inside.

"All right," she said. "But I'll still have to pass on the hamburger." There was no way she was going to spend the evening in his company. First she had to figure out how she felt about him.

"Okay," he agreed. "Another time."

Don't bet on it, she thought. She tugged her hand free, avoiding his eyes, and turned to go.

"One more thing," he said.

Ronnie stopped. What now? Didn't the man ever give up?

"I was dead wrong, you know."

Curiosity won out over Ronnie's better judgment. "About what?" She turned toward him.

He moved closer, and Ronnie held her breath. "You don't look eighteen at all," he said softly. "Right now, with your hair pulled up into those tails, and with those little beads of sweat on your nose . . ." He reached out, and with his thumb he rubbed at the end of her nose.

Ronnie's stomach curled with a liquid, warm feeling, and her breath came in shallow spurts.

". . . You look more like . . ." He paused, and a wide grin split his face. His eyes danced. "You look more like a sixteen-year-old!"

The next morning Ronnie was still trying to decide whether she couldn't stand Alex Summerfield or whether she hoped he was interested in her. There had been definite promise in his eyes as he'd waved her on her way the night before. But even if he were interested in her, it would be insanity to get involved with him. All he was probably looking for was a beach bunny to spend the summer with, and Ronnie had no intention of being anyone's beach bunny.

That had to be it, because he couldn't be seriously interested in her. She wasn't his type at all.

Ronnie grimaced as she ate her Rice Chex. It should be obvious to anyone that the type of woman Alex Summerfield would be interested in would be tall, classy, and elegant, with perfectly coiffed hair and long, red fingernails. Ronnie grinned as she looked at her own short, unpainted nails. Forget him, Valetti, she told herself, finishing her morning tea in one last gulp. Then she hurriedly cleaned up the kitchen so she wouldn't be late for work.

About ten o'clock that morning the first call of the day came through. On any given day in Juliette, there weren't a great many calls to the sheriff's office. An occasional domestic disturbance, or maybe some kids would get drunk and rowdy at the park and someone would report them, or maybe there would be a squabble between neighbors, but there was rarely anything more significant.

Not that there wasn't occasional danger on the job. Ronnie's first year as a deputy, someone had tried to hold up the gas station, and she'd proven her ability for cool thinking under fire when she'd chased the would-be robber, caught him, and subdued him all by herself.

Then there was the time a team of con artists tried to pull a scam in Juliette. Ronnie had been suspicious of them from the first. There were two of them: a man and a woman. The woman was a gum-chewing, brassy blonde. Her so-called husband was tall and handsome, but the two of them didn't seem like the kind of people who would stay in an out-of-the-way place like Juliette. They belonged somewhere like Saratoga and the racetrack.

So Ronnie had decided to investigate. When she'd quizzed Betty Brown, the owner of the bed and breakfast inn where they were staying, she'd found out Betty was about to invest her entire life's savings in a highly questionable stock deal the couple had convinced her would triple her money in no time at all.

But those kinds of incidents didn't happen often. The total population of Juliette was 2,365 people, and in the entire county there were only a little over 6,000 hardy souls. There were no main roads coming or going through the county, and the only people who knew Juliette existed were antique lovers. It was a nice place to live because of that, Ronnie thought. No murders, no burglaries, no excitement. Well, hardly any, Ronnie amended, as Alex Summerfield's dancing eyes invaded her memory.

She picked up the phone. Because William was on vacation and the other deputy working the day shift, Chuck O'Neill, was on traffic detail today, Ronnie would have to handle any calls that came in.

"It's Miss Agatha, sheriff," said Maisie as she put the call through.

Ronnie grinned. Miss Agatha, one of Ronnie's favorite people, was an institution in Juliette. She had been born and raised there, and to Ronnie's knowledge, had never had any desire to go anywhere else. Miss Agatha was at least eighty years old but didn't look it, and she was what used to be called a maiden lady.

"Veronica? Is that you?"

"Yes, Miss Agatha. It's me."

"Veronica, you must come right over to the shop. I've been the victim of a robbery!"

A robbery? Ronnie nearly fell off her chair. "You've got to be kidding," she said.

"Veronica, I would never stoop to making jokes about anything so serious," Miss Agatha said haughtily. "I am absolutely serious, my dear, and I need your help immediately."

"Sorry, Miss Agatha," Ronnie said. "Of course I'll come."

Ronnie couldn't wait to get there and hear Miss Agatha's story. She jumped out of her chair, then winced. Her muscles were sore today. A little more slowly, she picked up her beeper, strapped on her holster, told Maisie where she was going, and climbed gingerly into her car to drive the short distance to Miss Agatha's Antique Shoppe.

When Ronnie pulled into the small parking area in front of Miss Agatha's shop, she looked around. Everything looked exactly the same. Miss Agatha's family had owned the Victorian house since 1898. Gingerbready and ornate, it had a porch that ran all around the front and one side, and there were turrets and stained glass windows and numerous angles and curves.

Miss Agatha had turned the entire ground floor, except for the kitchen and pantry, into her shop and lived upstairs with her friend and helper, Hannah Richardson. Antiques spilled out onto the porch and side yard. Although Miss Agatha would never admit it, Ronnie thought the older woman made a pretty decent living from the shop. Her fame had spread, and now, especially during the warmer months, people had started coming from hundreds of miles away to look through her "finds." Ronnie liked to tease Miss Agatha and tell her she'd put Juliette on the map. The antique business was a thriving one in upstate New York.

Miss Agatha's screened door squeaked as she stood in the doorway watching Ronnie approach. Ronnie smiled as she saw her. Miss Agatha, a tiny bird-like woman, was always perfectly turned out. Today her white hair was coiled up into a neat topknot, tiny amethyst earrings were screwed into her earlobes, and a lavender flowered silk dress covered her small body. Miss Agatha favored shades of purple and seldom wore any other color. She stood with her ever-present ebony cane with the ivory handle gripped in her right hand.

"Good morning, Veronica," she said in a no-nonsense voice.

"Good morning, Miss Agatha." Ronnie climbed the three wooden steps up to the porch and shouldered her way around a dilapidated-looking cherry wood writing desk that blocked her way.

Miss Agatha led the way inside. Ronnie sniffed as she entered the wide entry hall. The smell of apples and cinnamon made her mouth water. "Ummm," she said, "is Hannah baking pies?"

"Yes. Would you like a piece?"

"I shouldn't," Ronnie said, "but I will."

Miss Agatha turned. Her sharp black eyes scanned

Ronnie's body. "Why shouldn't you? You aren't fat."

Ten minutes later, ensconced at the big walnut table in Miss Agatha's huge kitchen, a fragrant piece of hot apple pie in front of her, Ronnie listened to Miss Agatha's story while Hannah Richardson looked on.

"Then, Veronica, after looking around for perhaps a few moments, no longer, he coolly said goodbye and left." Miss Agatha paused dramatically. "It wasn't until a few minutes before I called you that I realized the brooch was gone."

Hannah, a tall, spare-looking woman with frizzy gray hair, nodded her agreement.

Ronnie frowned. "Describe this man for me."

Miss Agatha squinted as she stared off into space. "He's about six feet tall, I should think. Maybe not quite that tall. Perhaps only five-feet-eleven or thereabouts. Dark hair with streaks of silver running through it. Gray eyes. Strong-looking body. Very tanned. Good-looking face. Square and strong. A cleft in his chin. Well-spoken."

Oh, great, Ronnie thought. Unless Alex Summerfield had a double in Juliette, Miss Agatha had described him perfectly. "Miss Agatha, from your description of the man, I know who you're talking about. But I think you're mistaken about him being a thief. He's a famous playwright from New York City, and from what I know about him, he's very rich. He wouldn't steal from you." Ronnie wiped her mouth on her napkin. He might be conceited, but she'd bet her last dollar he wasn't a thief.

Miss Agatha frowned. Ronnie could tell she didn't believe her. "But, Veronica," she said reasonably, "the brooch has disappeared. No one else was here today. Even Hannah was out in the kitchen all morning."

"Are you sure the brooch was there this morning?"

"Positive. I saw it when I came downstairs. In fact, this morning I dusted the outside of the case it was in. That's how I'm so certain."

"Show me," said Ronnie.

Leaving Hannah in the kitchen, the two women walked to the front of the house and into what used to be the dining room. It was now crammed with every type of furniture imaginable, as well as antique jewelry, pottery, and knick-knacks of all kinds.

Miss Agatha walked straight over to a glass-enclosed case. She pointed through the glass to a spot in the middle of the velvet-covered table which was blacker than the faded cloth surrounding it. "See?" she said, dark eyes glittering. "You can see for yourself the brooch is no longer there."

"Well . . ." Ronnie hedged.

"Veronica," Miss Agatha said, "he is the only person who could have taken the brooch. No one else was here."

"How did he take it if you were in here the whole time?"

"I wasn't. That's the point. I walked across the hall to answer the telephone, leaving him alone in here." She smiled in satisfaction. "That's when he pocketed the brooch."

Just then, as if on cue, the phone rang, and Miss

Agatha excused herself, leaving Ronnie to speculate on the mystery of the missing brooch.

"Why, yes," Miss Agatha was saying, "I keep my shop open until six in the evening every day except Thursdays, when I stay open until nine. . . . Yes, it's easy to find. Come into the center of Juliette and take a right on Bishop Avenue. Yes, Bishop. My shop is about two blocks down on the left hand side. You can't miss it. That's Miss Agatha's Antique Shoppe, with two 'P's and an 'E.' "

Ronnie grinned. Two "P"s and an "E." She'd never heard Miss Agatha say it any other way. She heard the older woman hang up the telephone.

"How much was that brooch worth?" Ronnie asked as Miss Agatha returned. Why would Alex Summerfield take it?

"About seventy-five dollars," Miss Agatha said.

Surely Alex Summerfield could afford dozens of seventy-five dollar brooches. "Miss Agatha . . . are you sure about all this?"

Miss Agatha folded her arms in front of her. The sun slanting in through the window fell across her soft-looking skin. Ronnie could see the fine dusting of powder across her nose and the faint tinge of pink rouge she'd applied to her cheeks. She pursed her lips stubbornly.

Oh, darn, Ronnie thought. Miss Agatha wasn't going to budge on this. With a resigned sigh, Ronnie said, "All right, Miss Agatha. I'll go ask Alexander Summerfield about your brooch. But that's all I'm going to do. Ask him if he knows anything."

Miss Agatha smiled. "Thank you, Veronica. That's all I wanted—that you go talk to him."

Sighing again, Ronnie said, "I'll let you know what happens."

"And Veronica . . ."

"Yes?"

"Now don't get mad . . ."

Ronnie rolled her eyes. "Now what?"

"Don't you think you should put on some makeup and fix your hair before you go to see him?"

THREE

Alex's morning had been difficult. He got up early, intending to get started on the rewrite of Act II while his brain was still fresh. He'd always liked writing early in the day. But today he hadn't been able to concentrate.

Signposts. He'd been so excited when he'd first had the idea for the play. It was the story of a young man coming of age in modern-day America. He was faced with a monumental decision and torn by doubts. The premise of the story was that in each life there are signposts along the way, but sometimes people miss them or take the wrong road. Sometimes the signpost is so small and insignificant the person doesn't realize it is one, and they ignore it, thereby changing the course of their lives.

Alex knew that if he could only write the story the way he'd first envisioned it, it would be wonderful. Oh, yes, he thought. How simple it sounds. Just write the damned thing.

The trouble was, until three years ago, it *had* been

simple for him to write terrific plays. Every day he'd just sit down and do it. He'd been obsessed by his ideas and had always been able to push every other thought out of his mind and focus his entire being on the task at hand. Why had that ability deserted him? he asked himself for the thousandth time. And, as usual, Margo's face popped into his mind.

Margo. He'd been besotted by her. She had become his obsession, taking the place of his writing. From the moment Alex had laid eyes on her, he hadn't been able to think of much else. He'd fallen so easily into the trap of thinking it couldn't do any harm to take her to Cannes for a week. He would write twenty-four hours a day when they returned. Why not make her happy? But when they'd return, there would be someplace else Margo wanted to go, and Alex would find himself once more delaying the start of a new project. "Just a week, darling. Is that too much to ask?" Margo would plead, and he couldn't resist her.

Yes, she'd bewitched him. All he'd wanted was to be with her, see her smile, make her happy. But in the end, he hadn't made her happy. She'd left him, and ever since he'd been trying to pick up the pieces. She hadn't been a part of his life for nearly two years now. *Two years*. Certainly a long enough time for Alex to snap out of his lethargy.

Coming to Juliette had been a last ditch attempt to recapture the magic touch that had deserted him. And so far, it had worked. Until this moment, he hadn't once thought of Margo. No, he thought wryly. Instead of thinking about Margo, you've been thinking about a tiny brunette with huge blue eyes.

When he'd first seen her, he'd simply been intrigued by her and irritated with himself. Then, when she and Barzini had come to rescue the cat, he'd found himself amused and charmed. She'd seemed terribly young and vulnerable, entirely unsuited to the job of sheriff.

Then yesterday afternoon, when she'd run up the driveway, he'd been seized by desire at the sight of her in those short shorts and skimpy T-shirt. She was one sexy woman—her innocent-looking face a perfect foil for her delectably curved body. Alex smiled as he remembered her deliciously full lower lip and how it quivered when she was angry. For a moment yesterday, he'd been sorely tempted to pull her into his arms and kiss her until she was senseless. He smiled as he remembered the look of pure outrage on her face when he'd told her she looked sixteen years old. Sixteen, my foot. Lolita in a Stetson.

Good grief, Summerfield, he thought. Get Veronica Valetti out of your mind. Don't trade one female obsession for another! Haven't you learned your lesson yet? Women and writing plays don't mix. At least not for you.

And rehearsals for *Signposts* were starting in less than three months.

Alex stared at the paragraph he'd just typed. Garbage. That's exactly what it was. In frustration, he yanked the sheet of paper out of his typewriter, crumpled it up, and threw it into the already-full wastebasket. "Hell's bells," he said. He took off the steel-rimmed glasses he wore while working, pushed his chair back, stood up, and walked to the open window.

It was another gorgeous June day: cloudless, pure blue sky, cool air starting to warm up under the golden sunshine, birds chattering in the trees. This was a day he should be glad to just be alive. Rubbing his forehead, he decided to put on some music. Sometimes that helped him concentrate. Soon the lilting sound of Chopin filled the air, and Alex settled himself back down in front of the typewriter.

"Now," he said aloud, "put everything else out of your mind . . . especially the little sheriff. . . ."

Before he'd even finished the thought, he heard the sharp rapping of the knocker against the front door.

"Damn it," he swore. "Now what?" Striding rapidly to the hall, he yanked open the door. Standing outside his door, looking like a teenager playing dress-up in her khaki uniform and jaunty Stetson, stood Veronica Valetti, an uncertain smile on her face.

"Well," he drawled, "what have we here?" All his anger over the interruption to his work and all thought of his abandoned manuscript fled his mind.

"Hello, Alex," Ronnie said. She smoothed her hands over her hips in a nervous gesture.

He stood aside. "Come in," he said. She followed him into the bright living room and sat primly upright in one of the big wing chairs flanking the fireplace. She removed her hat, placing it in her lap.

Alex sat in the other chair, leaned back, grinned and said, "Does this visit mean you've forgiven me?"

"For what?" she asked, but there was a telltale hint of pink in her cheeks.

"You know what."

"If you're referring to the remark you made last night, that's not why I'm here."

He raised his eyebrows. "Well, what is it, then?" He snapped his fingers. "I know. You don't like Chopin."

She winced, and Alex wondered why she seemed so uneasy this morning. Surely she knew he was teasing her.

"What's the matter?" he said.

She bit her bottom lip, then took a deep breath. Alex watched in fascination as her chest rose, then fell. "Listen, Alex," she said, "were you in Miss Agatha's Antique Shoppe yesterday afternoon?"

"Yes. Why?"

"I got a call from Miss Agatha this morning, and . . . well . . . it seems as if a brooch is missing from her shop." The words tumbled out of her mouth in a rush, as if she had to hurry or she wouldn't say them.

"I'm sorry to hear that, but how does it concern me?" Alex watched as her thick brown eyelashes dropped to cover her eyes. The bright sunlight glinted on her shining hair, and he was struck by how utterly lovely she was. Sexy as well as sweet. A potent combination.

She ran her tongue over her lips, and Alex's hands tightened in his lap.

"Miss Agatha thinks you might have taken the brooch," she murmured.

"What?" Alex said incredulously. "*Me?*"

Ronnie raised her head, and now the pure blue of her eyes dazzled him. "I'm afraid so."

"But that's ridiculous! Why would I steal a brooch?"

"That's what I told her, but she insisted I come and talk to you. She said no one else was in the shop yesterday, and you *must* have taken it."

Alex chuckled. The accusation was so absurd it was funny. The old lady must have slipped her switch. And here he'd thought she was so interesting and intelligent when he'd met her yesterday. They'd had a fascinating conversation. She'd asked him all sorts of questions about himself, and he'd had the feeling she liked him. He must be losing his ability to judge people, because she'd certainly fooled him. He'd have been willing to bet money on her sanity.

"Well," he said, "you're welcome to search the house if you like. You won't find the brooch, though." Then, in a moment of pure deviltry, he added, "You can even do a body search, if you feel it's necessary."

Ronnie's face flamed red. She lifted her chin and stared at him.

Alex laughed. "Well, I wouldn't want to stand in the way of you doing your job properly."

She sat up straighter in her chair. "I know you're making fun of me, and in a way I can hardly blame you. It *is* a ridiculous accusation, but Miss Agatha accused you of taking the brooch, and as a law enforcement officer, it's my job to follow through and investigate the alleged crime." She said the words with dignity, and Alex's chest tightened. Without conscious thought, he stood up, walked slowly over to her chair, and reached for her hands.

She hesitated for a second, then placed her small

hands in his. He pulled her up. They were standing only inches apart. She swallowed as she raised her eyes to meet his. He could see the little pulse beating in her throat and smell the faint scent of roses on her skin.

Alex slid his arms around her, watching as her thick eyelashes drifted down, fanning across her cheeks. She fit into the nook of his arms as if she'd been made for him. He knew he was asking for trouble, he knew it was stupid, but he couldn't seem to help himself. His mouth lowered, and he whispered, "I'm not making fun of you, sheriff. I'm surrendering."

Ronnie was so stunned when Alex pulled her into his arms, she didn't even try to resist. All thought vanished from her mind, and her emotions took over. Sensations crowded her consciousness: the feeling of safety and strength his strong arms and body evoked, the musky scent of his skin, the heady jolt of joy that shot through her at the touch of his cool, firm lips, the lightheadedness that threatened to overwhelm her as the kiss went from a gentle brushing of their two mouths to a heated surge of mutual passion. Ronnie had never experienced a kiss that had shaken her so deeply.

When Alex gradually released the pressure of his arms and slowly broke the connection between their lips, Ronnie trembled with delayed reaction. She drew a deep, shaky breath and tried to pull away from him, but Alex held her in the loose circle of his arms and said huskily, "If this is what I have to look forward to as your prisoner, I may take up a life of crime."

"Please let me go," said Ronnie. She couldn't look at him. She felt exposed and too vulnerable to his charm. Forcing herself to keep her voice even and her feelings hidden, she raised her head and met his laughing eyes. Later, away from that amused gaze, she would allow herself to examine her feelings, but not now.

She turned away from him, and he dropped his arms. Smoothing down her uniform, she said briskly, "Now that you've had your fun, I think it's time I left." Lifting her chin, she said, "I'll inform Miss Agatha that you didn't take her brooch."

Ronnie was gratified to see the amusement disappear from his eyes and a slight trace of confusion pass over his face. "I wasn't making fun of you."

"Come on, Alex. Let's not play games. We both know why you kissed me. But there's no reason to worry about it. I've been kissed before. I know the score." She smiled and prayed the smile looked real. "Don't give it another thought." Then she turned on her heel and walked out of the room. She didn't look back.

Damn him, she thought as she drove back to her office. Angry tears welled into her eyes, and she furiously blinked them back. Why was she letting him get to her? She clenched her teeth. She'd show him she could be just as cool as he was. And really, what *was* she so upset about? It had just been a kiss. Not a declaration of undying love or anything. A simple kiss. Big deal. It'd be something she could laugh about some day. Something she could tell her grandchildren about.

"I was kissed by a famous playwright once," she'd say, and they'd all smile and think how dotty their grandmother was.

By the time Ronnie reached her office, she'd managed to recover some measure of equanimity. But for the rest of the day, her treacherous mind kept wandering back, conjuring up images and sensations she would have preferred to bury forever.

Now why the hell had he done that? What was it about Veronica Valetti that made him forget all his good resolutions? How many times over the past two days had he told himself that he wasn't going to become involved with her? She wasn't like the women in New York City—the beautiful actresses and models and other sophisticated women he'd dated after his breakup with Margo. They really did know the score. Sure, he'd shared some casual lovemaking with a few of them, but that's all it had been: casual. They had known it, and he had known it. He'd never made them any promises; he'd never treated the encounters as anything but what they were—a way to forget the hurt and Margo.

With each brief liaison, Alex had been careful to choose women who didn't want or expect anything more from him than he had been willing to give. As far as he knew, he'd never hurt anyone or used anyone. And he didn't want to start now. So he'd better be very careful. Because instinctively he knew that Veronica Valetti would never fall into the category of someone who would indulge in a casual love affair. That would not be her style. She was the type of woman who would never give any part of herself casually. So, if you knew that all along, he asked himself, why in the name of heaven did you kiss her?

Suddenly furious with himself, he grabbed a plump pillow from the couch and threw it against the wall, knocking over a lamp in the process. The base of the lamp shattered, scattering pieces of painted porcelain all over the shining hardwood floor.

Alex released a chain of invectives, and after he was through, he felt enormously better. Now he would owe Barzini compensation for the lamp. For the next half-hour Alex cleaned up the pieces of porcelain and chastised himself for his thoughtless action in kissing Veronica. No matter how irresistible the impulse, no matter how tempting she was, he should have steered clear of her. Thank God she had treated the incident lightly.

"She let you off the hook," he said aloud. "So take the opportunity presented and forget about this episode . . . and her." And, he thought, if he couldn't completely banish her from his mind, at the very least, he could control his baser instincts when he was in her company. He was a grown man, not a kid with overactive hormones. "So act like one!" he said, settling back down in front of the typewriter.

At two o'clock the phone on Ronnie's desk rang.

"Sheriff, it's Elmira Crutchins for you," said Maisie.

Ronnie moaned silently. Elmira Crutchins was the town busybody. "Put her on," she said. "Hello, Elmira, how are you today?"

"I'm fine. But I didn't call to gossip," Elmira said. "There's trouble over at the Jacobsens' house."

Ronnie sat up straighter. Elmira now had her full attention. "What kind of trouble?"

"I think Pete's at it again," said Elmira. "The noise coming from there sounds like somebody's throwing things, and I heard Laurie scream a minute ago. You'd better come."

The anxiety in Elmira's voice communicated itself to Ronnie. This was a part of the job she hated, but Laurie Jacobsen was a good woman, and Ronnie had to try to help her. Even if she wouldn't help herself, Ronnie thought. "I'll be there in five minutes," she promised.

Ronnie picked up her service revolver, checked it, then slipped it into her hip holster as she left her office on the run.

As Ronnie pulled up in front of the sagging front porch of the Jacobsens' frame house, she saw Elmira Crutchins emerge from her house next door. A smacking sound, then a loud crash followed by a woman's scream and the crying of small children carried clearly through the open windows of the Jacobsens'. Motioning Elmira to stay back, Ronnie squared her shoulders and walked purposefully up onto the porch and banged on the screen door. For a few seconds the sounds of battle continued; then Ronnie's hard knocking must have filtered through, because suddenly silence reigned inside.

Ronnie took advantage of the silence to shout, "Pete! Laurie! Open the door. This is the sheriff."

More silence, broken only by a child's whimper.

Ronnie tugged on the screen door, but it was latched on the inside. "Pete," she said more quietly, "if you don't open this door I'll cut the screen and come in anyway."

The soft threat worked because a moment later the wiry frame of Pete Jacobsen appeared on the other side of the door. "Whadda you want?" he snarled. Then he spied Elmira standing on the sparse grass of his front yard. "I shoulda known. Old nosy-britches herself!" As he unlatched the screen door he muttered, "Stupid old cow. Whyn't she mind her own business?"

"Never mind Elmira," Ronnie said firmly. She took in Pete's disheveled appearance—the lank blond hair, the stubble covering his face, the stained clothing, the strong smell of sweat and whiskey emanating from his body. "What's been going on here, Pete?" She pushed past him into the kitchen, where she found a shaken and trembling Laurie cowering in a corner with her two small children clinging to her legs. Her tearstained face sported several old black and blue marks as well as a bloody lip and swelling left eye.

Ronnie knelt beside Laurie. "Laurie," she said softly, "you're hurt."

"I'm all right," Laurie said. She brushed Ronnie's hands away. "Really," she said as she saw the disbelieving look on Ronnie's face. "I fell."

Ronnie clenched her teeth. She looked up at Pete. He looked perfectly confident his wife wouldn't say anything against him. And why shouldn't he? She never had before, and this kind of thing had happened many times. Too many times, Ronnie amended. "I see," she said to Laurie. "You fell." She stared at Laurie. "How? What caused the fall?"

Laurie's pale blue eyes darted nervously around the room. She stood up hesitantly, and Ronnie stood up, too. The two little boys still clung to their mother's legs. Both were too skinny and had frightened eyes. "I . . . I tripped over that truck over there. . . ." Her head nodded toward a rusty child's toy on the floor of the kitchen. "I . . . I c . . . cut my lip when I fell." She patted the head of her smallest boy.

Ronnie sighed and shook her head. She stared hard at Pete, and after a few seconds, his eyes dropped, unable to meet her accusing gaze. "You heard her," he muttered, "she fell." Then, gathering courage, he lifted his chin and said, "What's the big deal anyways? Huh? Why'd you have to come runnin' out here? This ain't no matter for the law. This is a private matter. Ain't that right, honey?" He glared at his wife as if daring her to disagree with him.

"Pete's right, sheriff. This don't concern you." Laurie patted the shoulders of her boys and met Ronnie's eyes levelly.

"Laurie, we've known each other a long time. Don't lie to me." Ronnie knew it was hopeless, but she had to try to persuade Laurie to do something to help herself. She turned to Pete Jacobsen, who stared defiantly at her. "Go outside for a minute, Pete." She inclined her head toward the back door. "I want to speak to Laurie alone."

"I don't hafta go anywhere," he said belligerently, but he inched his way toward the door as

Ronnie continued to stare at him. Finally he dropped his eyes, and still muttering, let himself out onto the back porch.

Ronnie turned back to Laurie. "Pete doesn't have any right to knock you around, Laurie. No man has a right to hit his wife. I don't care what happened, or why it happened. You don't have to put up with this kind of life." Seeing the obstinate, closed look on Laurie's face, Ronnie said desperately, "If you don't care about yourself, think of your children, for God's sake! They are obviously scared to death." Then, more quietly, she added, "Why don't you come with me? I'll find a place for you and the boys to stay for awhile. It'll give you a chance to think."

"My place is here with Pete," Laurie said stubbornly.

Ronnie sighed again. She shrugged her shoulders. "One of these days that husband of yours is going to do more than hit you. One of these days he may kill you in one of his drunken rages." She walked to the open back door. "Come back in, Pete." When he was once more in the kitchen, she asked in a scathing tone, "What happened this time? Did you get fired again?" Pete Jacobsen had lost one good job after another because of his uncontrollable temper and penchant for whiskey.

His upper lip curled. "I didn't get fired. I quit! I hated that job anyways."

The "hated" job was one Pete had been overjoyed to get only two months earlier.

"So how do you intend to take care of your family? Pay for food?" Ronnie asked.

"Don't you worry. I'll take care of 'em. I always

take care of 'em, don't I, honey?" His bloodshot eyes demanded that his wife bolster his claim.

"Yeah, Pete, that's right. You always take care of us," Laurie agreed. She walked to her husband's side and put her arms around him. He enfolded her in his arms and gave Ronnie a triumphant look. One little boy sucked his thumb noisily, the other sniffled and shuffled his feet.

"So go back where you came from, *sheriff*," Pete said. "You ain't needed here."

"Remember, Laurie," Ronnie couldn't resist adding, "if you ever need me . . . all you have to do is call. The offer of a place to stay is open. I'll help you."

There was no answer, but Ronnie hadn't expected one. She looked at the couple for a long moment, then turned and let herself out. Elmira Crutchins stood outside, her plump arms folded across her ample chest, an exasperated look on her shiny face. "That Pete Jacobsen is bad news. One of these days he's going to really hurt Laurie or one of them kids," she said.

"I know. Thanks for calling me, Elmira. You'll keep an ear open, won't you?"

Elmira nodded. "I'll call you if I hear them at it again."

"Thanks," Ronnie said and climbed into her car to go back to the office. The episode with the Jacobsens had upset her more than she wanted to admit. Why was Laurie Jacobsen so stubborn, so blind, when it came to her husband? Was she so afraid of life on her own? Ronnie closed her eyes for a moment, suddenly overwhelmingly grateful to her father, who had instilled a sense of confidence and pride in her that she knew no one would ever be able to diminish.

After lunch Alex decided to pay Miss Agatha Applewhite a visit. Maybe he could get to the bottom of why she'd accused him of stealing her brooch. He decided to walk. Her shop wasn't far, maybe two miles, and he could use the exercise. Dressed in a pair of faded jeans, a bright red T-shirt, and his faithful Nike shoes, he set out at a brisk pace. God, he loved this part of the country. It was beautiful. Everywhere he looked wildflowers sprouted, and the smells were clean, country smells—not filled with automobile exhaust and too many bodies crowded into too small a space. He took deep lungfuls of air and hummed under his breath as he strode along.

Before long he reached his objective. He smiled as he saw the white sign hanging in front of the shop. The intricate scroll said "Miss Agatha's Antique Shoppe" and looked just like the lady herself—fussy and feminine.

Alex bounded up onto the front porch and rapped on the screen door. Without waiting for an answer, he let himself in, then blinked at the sudden dimness of the entry hall. "Anybody home?" he called.

A tall, thin woman emerged from the doorway at the far end of the hall. She smoothed back her frizzy hair and said, "Yes? May I help you?" She wiped her hands on her apron as she advanced toward him.

"I was looking for Miss Agatha," Alex explained. "Is she here?"

"She's out back. I'll get her," the woman said.

While the woman went on her errand, Alex looked around appreciatively. He liked old houses, and this was a perfect example of a well-preserved specimen. He ran his hand over the smooth molding of the hall.

"Mr. Summerfield! What a pleasant surprise. I didn't expect to see you again so soon," said Miss Agatha as she entered the hall.

Alex grinned. The old lady, even if she was crazy, was as appealing in her own way as the sheriff was in hers. "Well, Miss Agatha," he said, "I had to come over as soon as possible to clear up this misunderstanding."

"What misunderstanding?" she asked. Her black eyes, shining with some emotion Alex couldn't identify, captured his. "Shall we go up to my sitting room?" she asked. "I'll ask Hannah to bring us a pot of tea and we can talk."

Bemused by her behavior, Alex nodded his agreement.

Ten minutes later they were comfortably seated in bright chintz-covered chairs around a low round table. The tall, thin woman, who had turned out to be Hannah Richardson, brought them a laden tray containing a steaming pot of tea, cups and saucers, spoons, wedges of lemon, sugar cubes, cream, and a large slice of apple pie, which Miss Agatha handed to Alex. After only token resistance, he succumbed to the savory aroma and took a bite. The pungent tang of tart apples was pure heaven.

"Now," Miss Agatha said after taking a sip of her tea, "what were we talking about?"

Alex stifled a smile. The old lady was playing with him, he decided, but to what end he had no idea. Well, he'd go along with her. She was amusing, and he could feel the strong force of her personality as she concentrated those sharply intelligent eyes on him.

"Miss Agatha," he said, "Sheriff Valetti told me you'd accused me of stealing a brooch from you. I wanted to discuss it with you. I didn't take your brooch."

"I know that."

Now Alex did smile. "Well, if you know that, why did you tell the sheriff I took it?"

"At the time I thought you did. Now I know you didn't," Miss Agatha said as if her statement explained everything.

"Oh," Alex said. He couldn't think of anything else to say.

"You see, Mr. Summerfield," Miss Agatha continued, a small smile lurking at the corners of her mouth, "I found the brooch this afternoon. It was sitting on top of my dressing table in my bedroom. I have no idea how it got there, but obviously, if it was there, you didn't take it, now did you?"

"No, I guess not." Alex ate the last bite of his pie and leaned back in his chair. On the surface her explanation seemed reasonable enough, but Alex couldn't shake the feeling that there was more to this than met the eye. His hunch that Miss Agatha had some ulterior motive, or was playing some kind of game, wouldn't go away. Well, he'd just have to wait and see what happened. That decided, he relaxed and set out to enjoy his visit with the charming old lady.

Thank goodness the day was almost over, Ronnie thought. When the telephone rang a few minutes before five, she cringed and crossed her fingers.

"It's Miss Agatha," said Maisie.

Ronnie grimaced. She'd forgotten to call the older woman after talking to Alex. She picked up the receiver.

"Veronica," said Miss Agatha's precise voice, "I'm very glad to have caught you before you left for the day."

"Oh, Miss Agatha," Ronnie apologized. "I'm sorry I didn't call you back. I *did* go to see Alexander Summerfield, and I should have called you to tell you what he said."

"That isn't why I'm calling, Veronica. No, I've found the brooch."

"You found the brooch! Why didn't you call me and tell me?" Ronnie asked.

"Veronica, it is not necessary to shout," the older woman admonished gently.

"I'm sorry." Why did she always manage to make Ronnie feel guilty about something?

"Yes, well," Miss Agatha said. "The brooch was simply misplaced. I found it in my bedroom."

Ronnie couldn't believe it. All that fuss over something that Miss Agatha had forgotten she'd removed from the case herself.

"No," Miss Agatha continued, "that's not why I'm calling. Mr. Summerfield visited me this afternoon to inquire into the matter of the brooch, and I assured him that the mystery had been cleared up."

Ronnie felt a surge of pleasure at Alex's thoughtfulness in going to visit Miss Agatha. Then she pushed it down. She reminded herself he was practiced in the art of seducing women, even old women. He just used different tactics with each. "I'm glad you found the brooch, Miss Agatha," she said. "And I'm glad you and Mr. Summerfield had a chance to talk. I always knew he didn't take your brooch."

"He may not have taken my brooch, Veronica, but he's definitely a scoundrel . . . and a thief."

Ronnie's eyes widened at the accusation, and for a minute she couldn't answer. Then she said, "Wha . . . what do you mean by that?"

"Just exactly what I said, my dear. A scoundrel and a thief."

"Does this mean you think he stole something else?" Ronnie said, unable to keep the incredulity out of her voice.

"Don't take that tone with me, Veronica. I'm not a child making up stories, you know." Miss Agatha's voice contained a chilling edge. "After all these years, you surely know me well enough to know I do not exaggerate or tell fibs."

That was true, Ronnie thought. Miss Agatha had never given her any reason to believe she didn't have her full faculties or that she imagined things. Ronnie sighed. Why couldn't this day have ended without this added problem? "What exactly did he take?" she asked.

"One of my Hummels."

OPENING ACT / 69

"One of your Hummels," Ronnie repeated inanely.

"Yes, Veronica, that is what I said. Why must you repeat things?"

Ronnie wished she could dig a hole and crawl into it. "Why do you say he took one of your Hummels, Miss Agatha?"

"Because while he was here we had tea together upstairs in my sitting room. I was called away to the telephone for a few moments, and when I returned he told me he had to leave. Later, when I went back upstairs I discovered the Hummel was gone. It was one of my favorites. The little newspaper boy."

Ten minutes later, as Ronnie drove toward home, she rehashed the conversation with Miss Agatha in her mind. Nothing Ronnie had said would dissuade the older woman in her adamant insistence that Alex Summerfield had pocketed her beloved Hummel figurine. In desperation, Ronnie had once again agreed to talk to Alex Summerfield. She didn't know what she'd say, or how, but she *had* promised.

"Veronica," Alex said as he opened his door thirty minutes later. "I'm glad to see you."

"Hello, Alex," Ronnie said. As she saw the appreciative glance he gave her, she was glad she'd taken the time to freshen up and change her clothes. She smoothed down the royal blue cotton jumpsuit, then hurriedly withdrew her hands as she saw his gray eyes follow her movements.

"I hope this means you won't hold this morning against me," he said.

"I told you not to worry about this morning," Ronnie said. "That's not the reason I'm here."

"Well, come on in," he invited and led the way into the living room.

Ronnie took the same chair she'd taken that morning.

"Would you like a glass of wine or some iced tea?" Alex smiled down at her, his gray eyes clear and bright.

Ronnie thought he looked extremely attractive in an open-necked green and white striped cotton shirt and a pair of baggy white cotton pants and soft-looking leather moccasins. The casual outfit seemed to suit his rugged good looks. "Wine sounds nice," she answered.

While he went off to the kitchen, she stretched her legs out in front of her and studied the room. Already she could see small personal touches of Alex's. There were books stacked on the walnut coffee table and a pair of steel-rimmed glasses sitting on top of some loosely piled papers on the sofa table.

"Here you are," Alex said as he entered the room and handed Ronnie a crystal wine glass filled with bubbly white wine. Alex took the chair opposite her and took a swallow from his bottle of beer. He crossed one leg over the other, not the way women do, but propping his ankle on his other knee in a very masculine pose. He studied her for a while, not saying anything, and soon Ronnie squirmed uncomfortably under his close scrutiny. "You look wonderful in that shade of blue," he said softly.

"Thank you." Still his eyes studied her.

"It makes your eyes look darker and it flatters your skin." When she didn't answer, he smiled lazily. "You *are* quite lovely, you know. In fact, I can't think why I thought you were so young. I must have been blind."

Ronnie stiffened. "Why don't you cut the bull, Alex? That line might work with all the other women you meet, but it won't work with me. I'm not upset over what you said yesterday or what you did this morning. I have more important things to worry about than what some bored playboy said or did."

At first he looked nonplussed by her unexpected attack, but then his eyes filled with admiration. Good, she thought. Alex Summerfield was entirely too confident of himself, too sure she would be an easy target. Well, no matter how attracted to him she was, she'd never give him the satisfaction of knowing it.

"I deserved that, too," he said.

The man was full of surprises. She took a swallow of her wine. "Now that we've got that out of the way, perhaps I can tell you why I'm here."

"All right," he said. He placed his bottle of beer on the floor and leaned forward. His eyes had an earnest look. "But before you do, will you please listen to me for a minute?"

Ronnie shrugged, but her breathing quickened. Damn him. He certainly could turn on the charm when he wanted to.

"I know we started out on the wrong foot, and I know it's my fault we did, but I really would like for us to be friends. Do you think we could forget about the past two days and start all over again?"

Ronnie stared at her glass of wine. Could she trust this man? More importantly, could she trust herself around him? She slowly looked up. He was smiling, but it wasn't a knowing smile. It was a sweet, inquiring sort of smile. A nice smile. Maybe, just maybe, he was for real.

Ronnie took a deep breath and said, "I'd like nothing better than for us to be friends, Alex, and I hope you'll still feel that way after I tell you why I'm here."

"Why don't you tell me then?" he said. The smile became broader, and his eyes twinkled.

"I'm afraid Miss Agatha thinks you've taken something from her again." When Ronnie saw his mouth open, she raised her right hand and said, "Wait. I know it's crazy, but she insisted I talk to you about it. She said when you went over there today to talk to her, you left with one of her prized Hummel figurines. I told her you didn't take it, but she wouldn't believe me."

Now the smile became a grin, then Alex laughed out loud.

Ronnie felt extremely foolish but was glad he was taking it so well. Then at his next words, she did a double take.

"Don't be so quick to judge Miss Agatha, Veronica," he said between chuckles. "This time she's right. I *did* take her Hummel."

FOUR

Ronnie's mouth dropped open, and her eyes widened. "You *did* take her Hummel?"

Alex's chest bounced with laughter, and his gray eyes sparkled. "That's what I said."

"But why? Why on earth would you steal Miss Agatha's Hummel?"

Alex lifted his bottle of beer and took a deep swallow. Then he said, "I didn't say I stole the Hummel. I said I took it."

"What's the difference? I don't understand . . ."

"I took it because the old lady is playing some sort of game with me, and I thought I'd stir the pot and have some fun with her . . . see what happens." His eyes took on a wicked gleam. "I'll tell you what. Why don't you tell her I'm a kleptomaniac, and we'll see what she says."

For a few moments Ronnie just sat there. The clock on the mantel chimed softly. Then she took a deep breath and said, "I think I'm going crazy." Either that, or everyone she knew was in a conspiracy to make her look and feel ridiculous.

Alex chuckled. "I know. I felt that way at first, too. But now I can hardly wait for tomorrow's episode. That's what we've got to do, you know. Think of this as the way you would a soap opera, with each day bringing a new installment, a new surprise."

Ronnie set her glass of wine on the coffee table and stood up. "You know, Alex, despite what you may think . . . I really do have serious business to attend to. I don't need to be running around on wild goose chases."

The smile teetered and almost disappeared. Almost.

"I'm sorry," he said. "I was just having a little fun."

"At my expense."

The look on his face reminded her of little Jason Traymore's when she'd caught him soaping her car windows last Halloween. Alex lowered his eyes. Ronnie wavered. She almost said, "It's all right, Alex. I'm not mad." But she forced herself to remain silent and wait.

Alex looked up. "I guess I didn't think about you when I pulled my little stunt. I really *am* sorry. Will you forgive me?"

When he spoke in that husky, intimate tone, Ronnie's insides felt like butter on a stack of pancakes. Calling on every ounce of her willpower, she kept her voice level and her face calm.

"Yes. But you've got to square things with Miss Agatha."

"I will. And I'll behave from now on," he said meekly.

"And," Ronnie added firmly, "you've got to promise me you won't stir up any more trouble with Miss Agatha. Specifically, that you won't take anything else from her shop. I don't want to have to come over here for the same reason again."

He raised his right hand. "Scout's honor."

Later, as Ronnie remembered the twinkle he hadn't been able to banish from his eyes, she wondered if she could believe him. Somehow she had the feeling Alex Summerfield would continue to disrupt her life one way or another.

The next afternoon Alex whistled as he stood outside Miss Agatha's door and knocked. He felt absurdly happy. For some reason he had been very productive in his writing this morning. In fact, he'd almost effortlessly come up with a solution to one of the problems he'd been having with a scene in the second act. If every morning went as well as this morning had gone, he'd easily have all his revisions done by the time Bernie came up at the end of July. At the very least, he'd have the second act finished and be well on his way to completing the third act.

Filled with a sense of wellbeing, he buried his nose in the bouquet of flowers he held in his left hand. The heady perfume of roses filled his senses, and he breathed deeply.

"Yes?"

Alex peered through the screened door. "Hello, Miss Richardson," he said cheerily. "Is Miss Agatha home?"

"Yes." She gave a disapproving sniff. "I'll call her."

Alex smothered a grin. The starchiness in the housekeeper's voice was a clear indication of her opinion of him. He shifted the two wrapped parcels under his arms and looked around. The profusion of furniture and odds and ends covering the huge porch delighted him, but he wondered what Miss Agatha did when it rained. A trickle of excitement ran through him as he waited. Miss Agatha and her eccentricities had given him the glimmer of a story idea.

The screen door creaked open. Miss Agatha, dressed in a white cotton dress covered with purple polka dots, said, "Good day, Alex. My goodness, are those for me?" Her dark eyes gleamed with pleasure.

Alex handed her the bouquet. "I come bearing gifts," he said, "and apologies. May I come in?"

"Of course." She turned, and he followed her into the entry hall. "Would you like to sit out on the back porch, or shall we go upstairs into my sitting room?"

"It's such a beautiful day; why don't we go outside?"

Miss Agatha led the way down the hall and through the enormous kitchen. Alex took a quick look around before following her brisk figure through the back door and onto the wide back porch. It, too, was full of furniture, but these pieces were placed in a cozy group inviting relaxation and conversation.

The grounds were covered with a profusion of tall elms, white birch, and maple trees. Pine trees in varying sizes dotted the broad expanse of green. Rose bushes, lilac bushes, boxwoods, and several varieties of evergreens Alex wasn't familiar with were planted helter-skelter around the yard. A large garden with already-tall tomato plants, tender new lettuce leaves, onions, carrots, and a smattering of other vegetables and herbs occupied the entire left side of the yard. A white gazebo sat saucily on a rise of ground to the far right. A large birdbath stood at attention in the middle of the yard. Several small birds chattered as they sipped and strutted around the lip of the bath.

"What a wonderful place!" he exclaimed.

Miss Agatha smiled. "Yes, I think so. Please have a seat."

Alex held out the two wrapped parcels. "Also for you," he said. Then he sank into a large wicker chair and sighed contentedly. Dozens of windchimes tinkled merrily as the soft breeze played against them.

Miss Agatha slowly unwrapped the smallest parcel and placed the white tissue paper on a large glass-topped wicker table. "Ahhh . . . I thought so. My little newspaper boy." She held the Hummel up to the light and admired the delicate blues and browns of the fine porcelain figurine.

"Yes, I'm sorry you were worried about it," he said. Then he waited for her to make the next move. But she made no other comment, just unwrapped the larger parcel and removed the slim book.

"*The Poetry of Elizabeth Barrett Browning*," she read. She raised her dark eyes, and Alex could feel the force of her strong personality as she captured his gaze. For a long moment neither one spoke. Then her lips curved in a knowing smile. "Thank you. I know I shall enjoy reading this."

Wasn't she going to ask him about the Hummel?

Her silence on the subject puzzled him, but Alex forced himself to stick to his plan of waiting until she questioned him about his motives for taking the figurine.

"Would you like hot tea, iced tea, or something stronger? I have a bottle of Glenfiddich."

Alex raised his eyebrows. The woman was full of surprises. "I'd love a glass of Glenfiddich. With just a little water," he added.

"Hannah!" she called.

Minutes later the housekeeper put a large crystal old-fashioned glass three-quarters full of amber liquid in his hand and a tall tumbler of iced tea in front of Miss Agatha, who had seated herself across from him.

"Now, where were we?" she asked.

Alex smiled. The old lady was certainly foxy, he'd give her that. Yes, she'd make a wonderful character in a play. "I didn't know we were anywhere," he hedged.

"I think you've just trumped my ace," she said slyly, "and now you have to explain why."

"Doesn't that depend upon whether we're partners or opponents?" Alex countered.

"We're not opponents," she said.

"Ahhh." A tiny germ of an idea poked into a recess of Alex's mind. "Then I don't know what to say."

"What did you tell Veronica?"

Alex considered saying, "About what?" Instead, he chuckled and said, "I just told her I knew you were playing some sort of game and had decided to throw a new element into the pot to see what happened." He watched her face as she considered his words. Her shrewd eyes sparkled, and there was a glimmer of a smile on her face. "You know," he said slowly, thoughtfully, "you're much too smart a lady to have misplaced that brooch. No, there's some reason you accused me of stealing, and I want to know what it is."

"I really have no idea what you are talking about," she said firmly. "But it *is* a great relief to know you only took the Hummel to see what I'd do. I would hate to think I had so misjudged you." She sipped at her tea. "Well, now that we have settled that matter, what shall we talk about next? Tell me your impressions of Juliette and the people here."

Alex considered pushing the subject of the brooch and the Hummel, but quickly discarded that idea. He'd find out Miss Agatha's motives when she was ready to expose her hand and not before. But he thought he now had a pretty good idea of what she was up to. He smiled and relaxed and passed a very pleasant hour in Miss Agatha's company. No other mention was made of the Hummel or her accusations.

Ronnie looked forward to Fridays. Although she was always on call, officially she didn't work weekends, and although she loved her job, she loved her free time, too. She could never understand people who were bored with life. To Ronnie, life was one long series of adventures, of interesting pastimes, of fascinating subjects to explore. Most of the time there weren't enough hours in the day to do everything she wanted to do.

But this particular Friday she couldn't shake the feeling of confusion and embarrassment caused by her visit to Alex Summerfield the evening before. Nothing had gone right since she'd met him on Wednesday. She hadn't felt this inept since she'd been fresh out of college and a rookie at her job. Everything about Alex Summerfield disturbed her: the way he looked, the way he acted, the way he made her feel, and the way their relationship had progressed. Progressed? What a joke. Regressed was more like it. Progression implied improvement. Instead, each meeting strained the threads of their fledgling friendship.

Ronnie sighed. No matter how much she thought about him or the events that had happened since she'd met him, nothing changed. She still felt foolish about the circumstances in which Alex had seen her. Except for their first meeting, Ronnie felt she had not shown herself in her best light. Investigating a catnapping, losing control of her temper, and running around accusing people of stealing—none of these incidents had been ones she was proud of.

Now she wondered if Alex Summerfield would ever view her as anything other than a joke. Well, she had no intention of letting him have another opportunity to poke fun at her. Although she wouldn't be able to avoid seeing him occasionally—after all, they lived only a few feet from one another—she would stay as far out of his way as she possibly could. Never mind her fantasies. Alex Summerfield didn't belong in her world.

With another heavy sigh, Ronnie bent over her

desk and put the finishing touches to her monthly report. She signed her name with a flourish, and just as she picked up the day's mail, the telephone at her left elbow buzzed.

"Sheriff?" Maisie's voice came clearly through the intercom.

"Yes?"

"Alexander Summerfield on line two."

A tiny leap of excitement coursed through Ronnie. She took a deep breath to steady her nerves, then picked up the phone and punched the button.

"Sheriff Valetti," she said briskly.

"And how's my favorite sheriff today?" His rich voice sent shivers down her spine.

"Busy."

"Then I'm really glad I called. If you're busy, that means you'll be tired tonight and you'll need relaxation, won't you?"

She thought she could hear a trace of amusement in his words but couldn't be certain. "I guess so," she said hesitantly.

"No guessing about it. It's a known fact that when you work hard during the day you must relax at night."

Ronnie smiled in spite of herself. "Says who?"

"Dr. Zummerfeeeld." His voice had taken on a thick European accent. "Dr. Zummerfeeeld prescribes for you ze relaxed dinner with a nice gentleman."

The smile stretched. Ronnie could feel it fill her face. "Oh? And who might that gentleman be?"

He dropped the accent and said, "Someone who feels his relationship with you hasn't gone exactly the way it should. Someone who feels he owes you a really nice, normal evening to show you he's not the unfeeling lunatic you probably think he is." Then his voice lowered. "Someone who likes you very much and meant it when he said he wanted to become friends."

Ronnie's heart refused to obey her silent command to be still. It raced around like an energetic toddler running from its mother. How could this man cause such turmoil in her body with a simple invitation? Ronnie hadn't felt like this since she'd been a teenager and madly in love with Mr. Winniger, her geometry teacher.

"What do you say?" Alex said.

"I . . . I'd love to have dinner with you."

"Good." He sounded pleased. "I'll expect you at seven." Without waiting for her reply, he hung up.

"Wait!" Ronnie called, but it was too late. He was gone. She'd been going to ask him where they were going so she'd know how to dress. Maybe she should call him back. Then she decided she'd just wear her new, much-too-expensive green silk dress—the one she'd told herself she could wear anywhere, which justified buying it.

Seven. She glanced at her watch. It was already four o'clock. Only three hours before she'd see Alex Summerfield again. And this time, she'd make sure she stayed in control at all times. They'd have a new beginning, and even though she knew nothing could ever come of it, Alex Summerfield would begin to see her in a different way.

* * *

At five minutes before seven, Ronnie put a small dab of Joy behind her ears and wrists and in the hollow of her throat, took one more look at herself in the mirror, and picked up her small black purse. Her palms felt clammy, and her breathing quickened as she carefully picked her way down the steps and walked the twenty feet to Alex Summerfield's door.

She picked up the brass knocker and listened to its loud clack as she let it fall against the plate. The sun had begun to lower in the west, and a golden glow suffused the evening sky. The smell of freshly mown grass drifted over the hedges at the edge of the gravel drive. Ronnie could hear Kathy O'Hara, her next-door neighbor, calling her children in for dinner.

The windows to the carriage house were open, and strains of Carly Simon's mellow voice floated through. Ronnie lifted the knocker and banged it down again.

The door opened. Alex stood in the doorway and smiled at her. "Come on in," he said. "You're right on time. I like that." His eyes traveled the length of her body, and Ronnie could see the approval in their gray depths. For a long moment his eyes held hers. An almost tangible undercurrent of electricity seemed to pass between them.

Ronnie swallowed, then wet her lips. Alex reached out and clasped her hands, pulling her inside at the same time.

"You look beautiful," he said softly.

"Thank you," she said. She thought he looked beautiful, too, but she didn't want to say so. Tonight he wore dark gray slacks and a soft-looking white shirt, open at the throat. Once again she could see dark, curly hairs poking through the opening. She caught the spicy scent of sandalwood and took a deep breath. She had an almost uncontrollable urge to touch him. Frightened by her strong feelings, she lowered her eyes.

Alex saw Ronnie look away suddenly. Her thick eyelashes lowered, and her body trembled slightly. God, she looked wonderful. He wished he could gather her in his arms and kiss her the way he had yesterday. The green dress she was wearing clung to her body and swayed gently around her legs as she moved. He could see the soft swell of her breasts in the deep "V" of the neckline and the rounded contours of her hips, the enticing curve of her small waist, and her firm little bottom as the dress adjusted itself to each of her movements.

As Ronnie moved past him and into the living room, he caught the subtle scent of roses again, as well as the clean, fresh smell of healthy girl. Alex felt the sudden tightening in his loins, and he mentally chided himself. He wasn't a teenager on his first date. Besides, he'd already decided to keep his relationship with Veronica Valetti strictly one of friendship. He cleared his throat. "What would you like to drink?" he asked as Ronnie placed her small purse on the coffee table and sat in the wing chair she seemed to regard as hers.

"What are you having?" She glanced at the half-full glass on the coffee table.

"Vodka and tonic."

"That sounds good. I'll have that, too."

"I'll be right back," he promised. "Don't go away."

She smiled and crossed her legs. The vivid emerald green dress glistened in the apricot glow of the setting sun. Carly Simon sang "Anticipation" as Alex moved to the makeshift bar he'd set up on the sofa table.

"Where are we going for dinner?" Ronnie asked as he handed her her drink.

Alex grinned. "We're not going anywhere. I cooked dinner for us."

"A man of hidden talents," she said. "I'm impressed." She hoped she'd managed to sound sophisticated, but the words of the song pulsed in her mind as tingles of anticipation darted through her body at the thought of spending the entire evening there . . . just the two of them.

"I've always liked to cook," Alex admitted. "I used to follow my Aunt Isabel around and beg to help her in the kitchen." He didn't mention that his aunt would never tolerate his help. He'd taught himself to cook in the years before he'd met Margo. Cooking had always soothed him. Anytime he'd get upset about something, he'd head for the kitchen.

"Did your aunt live with you?" Ronnie asked.

"No, it was the other way round. I lived with her."

"Oh?"

"My parents died in an automobile accident when I was only five," he explained. The old feeling, the one he'd thought he'd banished forever, suddenly flooded his mind. He still remembered the loneliness and the pain, the feeling that no one really loved him. He pushed the feeling down. "I was raised by my mother's older sister."

Ronnie saw the lost, hurt look in Alex's eyes when he told her about his parents' death. She swallowed against the sudden lump in her throat. "We have something in common then. I told you my mother died when I was only a baby. She had leukemia. But, of course, I still had Dad and my brothers." She picked up her glass and took a swallow of the cool, crisp drink.

"Tell me about your family," Alex said.

Ronnie could see he had regained control of his emotions. She settled back in her chair and said, "There's not that much to tell. Dad's dead now, too. He died almost four years ago. He was only fifty-four. I have two brothers—Chris, who's thirty-six, and Larry, who's thirty-eight. Chris is a veterinarian and lives in Schenectady with his girlfriend, Michelle. Larry is a systems programmer and lives in Albany with his wife and children." She grinned. "Then, of course, there's Sam and Miss Agatha, both of whom think they're surrogate parents or something."

"I figured as much," Alex said. His eyes twinkled. "I don't think Sam likes me much."

"Oh, don't pay any attention to him. Sam's like an old lady in a lot of ways. And you have to admit you didn't exactly endear yourself to him when you imprisoned Hector."

"True." Alex drained the last of his drink. "I have to check the steaks." He stood up.

"Need any help?" Ronnie asked.

"No, but you can come watch."

Ronnie followed him out to the tiny, modernized

OPENING ACT / 87

kitchen. She leaned against the doorframe and watched as Alex quickly and efficiently turned the steaks under the broiler, tossed the salad and sliced the French bread. Then she helped him carry everything into the small dining room.

The small round table looked lovely, with a bowl of fresh flowers in the center and two tall candles in silver holders. Alex lit both after seating Ronnie.

Although dinner was delicious, Ronnie felt too jumpy to eat much. Alex had prepared something he called double baked potatoes filled with a mixture of potato, cheese, and onions, and the thick New York strip steaks were broiled to perfection, but she was too unsettled by her strong attraction to him to do justice to the food. She noticed Alex didn't seem to have any difficulty finishing his portions, though.

"Would you like your dessert now, or later?" he asked.

"Why don't we wait awhile?" she suggested.

"Good idea."

"I'll help you clean up."

"No," he said. "We'll just leave the dishes. I'll clean up later."

"I insist." Ronnie pushed back her chair and stood. She stacked her plates and picked them up. "Come on. It'll only take a few minutes."

She walked out to the small kitchen. It looked very clean and neat. She couldn't believe he'd prepared dinner without leaving a mess. She never seemed to be able to manage that. "It's too bad you don't have a dishwasher," she said.

"I don't mind," he answered. "I don't generally dirty many dishes."

Ronnie filled one side of the double sink with hot water and added a generous dollop of liquid soap. She began to wash, and Alex dried and put the dishes away. Because the kitchen was so narrow, he brushed against her several times as they worked. Each time Ronnie felt the same charge of tension and electricity she'd felt earlier in the evening. It was hard to keep her voice level as they talked. She wondered if he felt the currents, too. She felt lightheaded, suspended in air, as if any moment she'd come crashing down to earth.

Later, as they sat over chocolate mousse and coffee, Alex began to tell her about his new play.

"I'm having some difficulty with it," he admitted. A lock of dark hair had fallen forward, and he brushed it back.

"What kind of difficulty?"

Alex shrugged. "Oh, different things. It's hard to explain, and you'd probably just be bored."

"Oh, no. I'd love to hear about it. I can't imagine how anyone sits down and writes a play. I'm fascinated."

Alex smiled, and Ronnie's heart caught. In that moment he didn't look sophisticated or arrogant or any of the things she'd first thought about him. Instead he looked pleased at her interest and . . . sweet. Sweet? Ronnie couldn't believe she had actually come up with the word *sweet* in connection with the great Alexander Summerfield.

"One of the problems I'm having is that I know what I want to happen at the end of the second act, but I'm not sure about the right way to get there."

He leaned forward, earnestness tinging his words. "See, it's important to foreshadow, let the audience get a glimmer of what will happen, so that when it actually *does* happen it isn't so much of a surprise that they don't believe it. Foreshadowing takes careful planning."

"I never realized—"

"No, of course not. Why should you?"

"Well, what is it you want to happen?"

"It's hard to explain if you haven't read what's taken place up to that point in the story."

Ronnie smiled. "Would you let me read it?"

"Uh . . ." He hesitated, his eyes narrowing. "I usually don't let anyone see my work . . . well, no one except Bernie, my agent."

"If you don't want me to read it, that's all right." She shouldn't have asked. She could see she'd made him uncomfortable.

"It's not that—"

"Really, Alex. I understand. I shouldn't have put you on the spot like that. I don't know anything about it. You're right not to trust me."

"I—"

"No. Don't apologize. I'm the one who should apologize. It's your work."

He studied her for a long moment. Ronnie could see the conflicting emotions on his face. "Maybe I *should* let someone completely fresh and objective take a look at it. Bernie and I have gone over this stuff so many times, I'm not sure either one of us is capable of seeing anything new." He stood up. "I may regret this, but I *do* want you to read it. The only thing is, I don't have any extra copies. I'll have to give you my working copy."

"I'll take very good care of it," Ronnie said softly. A warm glow suffused her at the thought of the trust Alex was placing in her. She thought she understood his feelings. What he was about to give her was a part of himself, and he didn't even know her. At that moment, Ronnie felt very special.

"I know you will."

A few minutes later he returned with a three-ring binder. He handed it to her, then sat down again. She glanced at the binder, noticed the dogeared pages inside, then set it on the coffee table.

"I'm excited about reading it," she said. "I'll try to have it back to you in a day or so."

"There's no hurry," he said. "I only gave you Act I and the first part of Act II—just enough so you'll know what I'm talking about. I kept the part I'm working on now." Suddenly he was very glad he'd given her the play to read. "I think I made the right decision in coming to Juliette for the summer."

"Juliette's a nice place to live," she said. She drained her coffee cup, then placed it on the coffee table next to the binder. "Peace, quiet, no distractions."

"Peace, quiet, and no distractions, huh?" *Except for you, pretty lady. You're a definite distraction.* As soon as the thought formed, Alex knew it was true.

"Well . . ." She stood up. "On that note, I'd better be going. It's getting late, and you're a working man."

"But tomorrow's Saturday," he protested. He didn't want the evening to end. He hadn't felt so relaxed, so easy around anyone except Bernie, in years.

"No rest for the wicked," she teased. "Don't writers work seven days a week? And didn't you just tell me you have problems with your play? No distractions, remember?"

Alex loved the mischievous smile on her face and the look of deviltry in her beautiful eyes. He stood up and walked around the coffee table. He reached out and with the tips of his fingers he touched her cheek, tracing the outline of her cheekbone. He felt the tremor in her body, and an answering tremor shook him. Her skin felt like satin against his hand, cool and smooth and lovely. His fingers moved under her chin, and he lifted her head. A faint pink stained her cheeks, and her breasts rose and fell rapidly.

"You're definitely a distraction," he murmured. "A beautiful, sexy, desirable . . . distraction." He saw the quick leap of pleasure in her eyes. What am I doing? he wondered. He'd meant to keep it light and friendly. "Good thing I've got a lot of willpower," he said.

"Yes," she whispered. "Good thing."

Alex called on every ounce of that willpower as he forced himself to drop his hand, to move back, to smile.

"It was a wonderful evening, Alex," she said. "Thank you for asking me."

"The pleasure was all mine," he said inanely. He knew he wouldn't be able to sleep that night. He might tell himself he wasn't going to get involved with Veronica Valetti, but the plain fact was he already was. And he wanted her. He wanted her badly. But we don't always get what we want, do we? he asked himself. Remember that, Alex old boy. Each thing we want carries a price tag. He must keep reminding himself of what had happened the last time he'd allowed a woman to become too important to him. Was he willing to risk the loss of his peace of mind again and in turn the loss of his ability to write?

They walked outside together. The air felt cool on Alex's skin, and the good summertime smells surrounded them. Crickets sang, and somewhere off in the distance a dog barked. The moon shone full and bright, and the navy night had a magical feel.

"Goodnight, Alex," she said as she turned to face him.

He knew she expected him to kiss her, and he wanted to . . . he wanted to more than he'd wanted anything in a long time. But he kept thinking about that price tag; and, full of regret, he backed away and said softly, "Goodnight, Veronica."

He turned and walked away.

FIVE

Ronnie floated through the ensuing weeks in a kind of golden haze. After that first dinner together, she and Alex fell into a comfortable routine. Each day Ronnie would go to work and take care of the hundreds of details and problems her position entailed, and Alex would work on his play. Sometimes Ronnie would catch herself daydreaming about him, but most of the time she managed to concentrate on her work, knowing she'd probably spend the evening with Alex. The knowledge that they were friends, that their relationship became more cemented with each passing day, that he depended upon her companionship and advice, that he was beginning to respect her opinions and views, that he trusted her enough to begin reading the day's work to her each evening and wanted her suggestions and feedback: all these were enough.

They discovered they both enjoyed almost every kind of music, from classical to pop to rock to bluegrass to country. Alex had brought his extensive collection of records up from the city, saying he knew he couldn't spend a summer without them, and Ronnie had been an avid collector for years. Many evenings they would sit and listen to Rosanne Cash or James Taylor or Bruce Springsteen or Whitney Houston and discuss the merits of this or that song, or this or that rendition.

On Tuesdays and Thursdays they'd jog together. Each admitted to the other how much they really hated running, but each agreed that the activity was a necessary evil in their lives. Alex told Ronnie how small and physically inactive he'd been as a child, how his classmates had made fun of him when he was a teenager because he preferred to stay inside and read rather than play basketball or touch football or baseball. Ronnie could picture the young Alex with his underdeveloped physique and shy, sensitive nature, and her heart felt squeezed by a huge fist as he related in a neutral voice how many jeers and indignities and hurts he'd suffered through at the hands of his peers.

"When I was sixteen I finally realized I had to do something about my life," he said. Ronnie could tell by the absence of emotion in his voice just how painful those growing up years had been. "I had to have a tantrum to convince Aunt Isabel that spending the money for a weight bench and other workout equipment wasn't throwing away money, but she finally agreed. After that, I worked out every single day until I was no longer the brunt of jokes."

Ronnie wanted to put her arms around him, but she didn't. She and Alex were maintaining a very careful distance; there was a line between them that neither seemed willing to cross just yet. Alex hadn't tried to kiss her once, hadn't put his arm around her or touched her except in the most casual way. Sometimes Ronnie wondered if he really didn't feel the tension and awareness and electricity in the air between them.

But she respected his obvious decision to ignore it, to keep their relationship one of close and valued friendship without sexual overtones. Deep down, Ronnie knew this course was wisest. At the end of August, Alex would leave Juliette, and she would never see him again. But some small part of her ached inside, a part she managed to keep deeply buried except for occasional bursts of hunger and need, even though she knew the situation wasn't going to change, even though she told herself not to be a fool.

During this period, an incident happened to reinforce the knowledge that this was a go-nowhere-but-friendship relationship. Ronnie and Alex had decided to take a picnic lunch down to a small park by the Juliette River, intending to spend the afternoon there. Alex had enthusiastically gone along with Ronnie's plans, telling her he made the best fried chicken in the world, and that that would be his contribution to the lunch. "I'll also furnish the beer and wine."

"Okay," she said, "I'll bring everything else." She unearthed a big wicker picnic basket from her mother's things and packed it with French bread, cheese, a jar of Kosher pickles, a container of potato salad she'd bought at the supermarket, brownies from the Juliette bakery, and a couple of crisp apples. Cooking wasn't Ronnie's strong point.

She found an old quilt they could spread on the ground and threw it on top of the steadily growing pile of stuff for the picnic. A Frisbee and Mary Higgins Clark's latest book joined the quilt.

Alex laughed when he saw all the things she had ready to be put in the trunk of the car. "We're only going to be there one afternoon," he teased.

"I like to be ready for anything," Ronnie said.

It was a beautiful, hot day with clear skies and a stiff breeze. The leather seats of Alex's car burned Ronnie's thighs as she slid in. "I should have worn jeans," she complained.

"I like you in shorts," Alex said as he started the car. He gave her an appreciative glance, his eyes lingering on her tanned legs in pink shorts.

Ronnie felt that queer, lighter-than-air feeling Alex always managed to produce in her when he looked at her in that lazy way. *Veronica Valetti, you're a fool. This is just a friendship, a summer flirtation with a gorgeous man, something to write about in your diary and remember when you're old and fat and have ten kids. This is nothing to build your hopes on.*

When they reached the park, they unloaded their things, and Alex spread the quilt in the shade of a leafy maple tree. The river sparkled under the bright noonday sun, and the air felt heavy with rich summertime smells. Ronnie sighed deeply and sat with her back supported by the trunk of the tree. Alex lay next to her, his head propped up on his arm, and he looked up at her. Ronnie turned her head, and something painful squeezed her heart as she looked into Alex's clear gray eyes.

Oh, God, she thought. He was so handsome. He was dressed in dark blue shorts and an open-necked white T-shirt. His arms and legs were tanned and muscular. He'd kicked off his sneakers, and he was wiggling his bare toes.

For a long moment, their gaze remained locked. A bee droned nearby, working at a patch of clover. In the distance, the shouts of children on the swings and seesaws carried clearly in the country air. Still holding her eyes, Alex reached over and lightly touched her hand.

"It's going to be hard to leave Juliette," he said softly, rubbing his thumb against the back of her hand. "I'll miss you."

The knot in Ronnie's chest grew tighter. Her heart thudded painfully as she struggled to keep her voice light. "I'll miss you, too." She forced a smile to her lips, but knew the smile was wobbly and prayed Alex wouldn't notice.

"We've had a lot of fun together, haven't we?" he said. She nodded.

"You're very different from the women I meet in New York. I feel much more relaxed around you. You're so natural and easy to be with."

"I'm glad." *Oh, Alex*. The part of her that had remained buried most of the summer pushed its way to the surface of her feelings, and she swallowed. Tears clogged her throat. She could feel herself falling apart, splintering into millions of pieces, and she knew she was very close to making a complete fool of herself.

She jumped up, avoiding his eyes. "It doesn't pay to get too relaxed, though. That leads to fat bodies and lazy minds! Come on." She grabbed at his hand. "Let's go throw that Frisbee."

The bad moment passed, but then, late in the day, after they were both sated with chicken and potato salad, and both were mellow from wine and sun and fresh air, Alex said, "Ronnie, have you ever been in love?"

They were both laying on the quilt, on their backs, looking up through the dark leaves at the filtered sunlight.

"Once."

"What happened?"

"Oh, we were both awfully young. He wanted to get married. I wanted to go to college. He was upset because he couldn't understand why. We broke up, and he joined the army. The last I heard he was stationed in Hawaii." Once, Tony's desertion had hurt, but now Ronnie felt as if she were telling the story about someone else. "He's probably married to some beautiful island girl by now."

"You don't sound unhappy about it," Alex said.

She turned her head to look at him. He was chewing on a blade of grass, and his sharp, clear profile looked like a dark paper cutout in the brilliant light.

"I'm not," she said. "It was a long time ago."

"How long does it take to get over someone you loved?"

Something in his voice told Ronnie this wasn't an idle question. She knew he was divorced. He'd mentioned it casually, once, but he'd never volunteered any other information, and she hadn't wanted to pry. "It took me about a year," she admitted. "Even then, I'd still think about him a lot, but it wasn't painful like it was at first."

"I think falling in love is not all it's cracked up to be. It takes too much emotional energy. Energy that would be better used someplace else."

He'd been hurt. Ronnie knew it. He didn't have to tell her. His words gave him away. Maybe he'd never admit it, but his ex-wife, or someone, had hurt him deeply, and he still wasn't over it. *That should tell you something, Valetti. Don't kid yourself into thinking that he's going to fall in love with you, because he's telling you, in plain English, that he's not. He doesn't want that kind of relationship, that kind of commitment.*

But she couldn't resist saying, "You must have been in love once, too. After all, you were married."

"I thought I was."

The words were clipped, and they didn't invite further comment. Still Ronnie pressed. "What happened?" He'd asked her, hadn't he?

"Nothing that doesn't happen a hundred times a day. I realized I'd mistaken good old-fashioned male hormones for something else." He rolled over and stood up in one graceful, economical motion. "I think we should start back, don't you?" All the way home Ronnie kept remembering the way Alex had refused to talk about his ex-wife. The only conclusion she could draw from that afternoon's conversation was that he was still in love with her. If it had *really* been a case of male hormones, or lust, or whatever name he wanted to call it, he wouldn't have minded talking about her. In fact, he would have laughed about it. People didn't have that hard, flat edge to their voices—they didn't avoid your eyes— when they were over something like that. That was it. Alex wouldn't, couldn't, talk about his ex-wife because what had happened still hurt him. And if it still hurt him, that meant he still loved her.

After the picnic, Ronnie tried to keep her feelings under control. She knew she was falling in love with Alex, but she tried to keep the knowledge buried, as if by keeping it repressed it wouldn't really be true. But sometimes, lying in her bed at night, she couldn't ignore the feelings any longer. It was times like those when she'd indulge herself and allow herself to dream. And the dream was always the same. She and Alex would become lovers.

Then some miracle would happen—something that would keep him in Juliette forever. But she knew this would never happen. No. What was far more likely was that Ronnie would be more in love with Alex than ever, and he'd still leave—taking her heart with him and leaving her nothing but memories.

But at least I'd have the memories, she argued with herself. Then she'd think: maybe he doesn't feel the same way I do. Maybe it was all her imagination— this tension—this hunger she sensed between them. This uncertainty about his feelings and her own fear of the future kept her from trying to change their relationship.

She told herself it would be too hard to see him leave if they became lovers—this way would be easier. But each day the awareness grew, the tension built, the electricity intensified, until Ronnie felt like a rubber band stretched almost to its limit, and she wondered how much longer she could stand the status quo. The rubber band was sure to snap; the only question remaining was, when?

One evening toward the end of July, as Ronnie climbed out of her car, she saw Sam walking toward her. The day was very hot, and Ronnie felt sweaty and dirty and tired. She couldn't wait to get upstairs and take a shower and have a cool drink, and she was anxious to see Alex. She knew he'd been working on Act III today, and she was excited to hear what he'd done. But Sam had a purposeful look on his round, flushed face, and Ronnie sighed inwardly. What now?

"Hi, Ronnie," he said. "I haven't seen much of you lately."

"Hi, Sam," she answered brightly. "I'm sorry. I've been really busy the past few weeks."

Sam's dark eyes slanted toward the carriage house. "I've noticed."

Ronnie tensed. "Yes, well . . ." she said.

"I . . . I've missed you," Sam said, turning toward her. "I've missed our games."

Sam and she had played weekly gin rummy games for years. Ronnie felt a guilty twinge as she realized she hadn't visited Sam in over a month. And he'd been so good to her for so many years. It's a wonder he's still speaking to me, she thought. In a spurt of contrition, she said, "Why don't you come upstairs with me? I'll fix us a cool drink, and if you don't mind giving me a few minutes to take a shower, then we can talk."

Sam smiled his agreement, and Ronnie led the way to her apartment.

Twenty minutes later, feeling cool and refreshed after her shower and dressed in white shorts and a blue and white cotton shirt, Ronnie wriggled her bare feet and took a long swallow of her wine spritzer. "Ahhh," she said with a contented sigh, "that tastes good."

Sam leaned forward across the kitchen table and said, "Ronnie, there's something I've got to talk to you about."

"So talk."

"Promise you won't get mad."

Ronnie glanced up. Sam had his motherly look again. Ever since the death of her mother, Sam, who had always been more than a cousin, had seemed to think he had to fill that role. And Tom Valetti, Ronnie's father, had indulgently allowed Sam to do it. She sighed. "I promise I won't get mad," she said. Let's get it over with, whatever it is, she thought.

Sam wet his lips and twisted his hands together, both certain giveaways that the matter he was about to introduce made him nervous about Ronnie's reaction. Ronnie braced herself. Somehow she was sure Sam wanted to talk about Alex.

"I know it's probably none of my business . . ." he began. Ronnie smothered a smile.

"But," he continued, "I couldn't love you more if you were my own sister or daughter, Ronnie. You know that."

She did know it. That's why she put up with these periodic lectures.

"And I'm really concerned about the time you're spending with our neighbor."

"You mean Alex?" Ronnie asked innocently. Sam continued to twist his hands together. Suddenly feeling sorry for him, Ronnie said, "Quit wringing your hands, Sam. Relax. Just spit it out. I won't bite you or anything." She grinned, but Sam didn't smile.

"Ronnie, I know it's easy for a young girl like you to be dazzled by somebody like Alex Summerfield. He's handsome, rich, and successful, and he's paying a lot of attention to you. But, Ronnie, he's not your kind. He's going to use you while he's here, but at the end of August he's going to leave. And you'll probably never hear from him again."

"I know that, Sam," Ronnie said gently, touched by the quaver in his voice. She reached across the table and patted his hands. "We're just friends. There's nothing for you to worry about."

"I wish I could believe that."

Ronnie smiled softly. "It's true. I realized from the very beginning that the only relationship Alex and I could ever have would be one of friendship, and that's exactly what it is—a friendship."

"Men like him won't be content to leave it that way," Sam said, a stubborn glint in his eye.

"You don't know Alex like I do."

"I know all I want to know."

"Sam, that's not fair. You're judging him on appearances. He's nothing like you imagine. He's sweet and warm and caring and sensitive."

"Huh!" Sam snorted. "He's got you snowed, hasn't he?"

Ronnie clenched her teeth. She'd put up with a lot from Sam, but enough was enough. "Okay. You've expressed your concern, and I appreciate it, but I'm twenty-nine years old, Sam. Old enough to pick my own friends and decide who I want to spend my time with."

"I'm sorry, Ronnie. I can't help it. I don't want to see you get hurt."

"I won't get hurt. I told you. My eyes are wide open."

"Why'd his wife desert him if he's so wonderful?"

"What?" Ronnie said in disbelief.

"There must be something wrong with him. They were only married a year when she left him," Sam mumbled.

"Who told you that?"

"I read it somewhere."

Sam was a devotee of the tabloid newspapers sold at the grocery store checkout counter, and this fact had in the past amused Ronnie. Now it didn't seem quite so funny. "Those articles you read are mostly garbage, and you know it," she said.

"Her name was Margo McKenna, and she's gorgeous. I saw a picture of her. She has red hair and brown eyes, and she looks like a movie star."

Ronnie didn't want to hear the rest, but like a child who watches a scary movie, she couldn't stop herself—or him. Alex had steadfastly refused to talk about his ex-wife. The only time he'd even mentioned her was that day by the river. Until this moment, Ronnie hadn't even known her name.

Sam was still talking. "And she left him and went to Europe, and no one knows what happened. She wouldn't talk about it, and he wouldn't talk about it." He took a breath. "There's something fishy about the whole thing."

Ronnie's patience snapped. She jumped up. "That's enough, Sam. I refuse to listen to another word. Alex is my friend, and I won't listen to this gossip."

"I knew you'd be mad." Sam stood, too. "I'm sorry if I've upset you, Ronnie, but I had to tell you. I just wish you'd think about what I said."

And Ronnie did think about it. Especially when, a few days later, she met Bernie Maxwell for the first time. When she came home from work that day, she saw a big blue Cadillac Seville parked in front of the carriage house.

Alex and she were supposed to go out for dinner that evening, and Ronnie hoped his company hadn't changed his plans. She thought about knocking on Alex's door before she went up to shower and change, then decided against it. Another hot day had left her feeling sticky and miserable, and she didn't want to meet anyone until she felt better. And looked better, she added.

At seven o'clock, dressed in a pale yellow sundress and matching yellow sandals, she walked over to Alex's and knocked. A few minutes later Alex opened the door.

The familiar tightening in his gut gripped Alex as he greeted Ronnie. Each day it became harder to resist her charm and appeal. She looked so fresh and pretty and delectable standing there in her sunny dress and lightly tanned shoulders and arms, with her hair shining in a just-washed look and her enormous eyes full of curiosity and happiness. Lately he'd begun to wonder why he even tried to keep their relationship from developing into a more intimate one. Lord knows, that's what he wanted, and he hoped that's what Ronnie wanted, too. His awareness of her grew stronger every day. She seemed to fill his thoughts even when she wasn't there physically, but the strange thing was, thinking of her didn't prevent him from writing. Just the opposite. His writing had never been better. All the reasons he'd had for not getting involved with Ronnie had seemed to evaporate, but still he held back. He knew now that his initial instinct about her was true. She wasn't a girl who would love lightly. Ronnie would give her all, and she would expect him to do the same.

But when she smiled up at him, as she did now, his heart did flip-flops, and he felt like a young kid, like anything was possible.

"Hi," he said softly, putting his arm around her shoulders and drawing her inside.

"Hi." There was an attractive pink flush on her cheeks, and she smelled like soap and roses and sunshine.

"How was your day?" he asked.

"Great," she said. "How was yours?"

"Terrific." He squeezed her shoulders, then dropped his hand. Touching her was dangerous, and the feel of her warm skin, firm and smooth, sent that charge of energy between them, crackling and vital and almost irresistible. "Guess what? Bernie's here."

"Your agent?"

"Um hum. Come on in. I want you to meet him."

Bernie Maxwell looked up as Alex and Ronnie entered the living room. Alex introduced them and watched as they appraised each other. He wondered what Bernie was thinking. The older man put his ever-present cigar into the ashtray Alex had found earlier and extended his tanned hand to Ronnie. His dark eyes gleamed.

"Nice to meetcha," he said. "Alex told me you live in the big house."

"Yes," Ronnie said. "Upstairs."

"Can't believe you're the sheriff of this burg. Too pretty and too young."

Ronnie smiled, and Alex chuckled. Bernie didn't have much finesse. When he thought something, he said it. "You'd better watch it, Bernie," he cautioned. "I almost blew my chances of being Ronnie's friend when I said something similar to that the first time I met her."

"Oh? You one of those women's libbers?" Bernie asked.

"No. Not really. But I *do* get sick of people thinking my appearance has something to do with my abilities."

By now the three of them were seated, and Alex pointed to his bottle of beer in a silent question to Ronnie.

"I'll just have my usual," she said.

Alex saw the faintly imperceptible lift of Bernie's eyebrows and the look he shot Alex's way. Alex wished he could say, "Don't worry, Bernie. Everything's under control." But he didn't. He got up and poured Ronnie a glass of white wine instead.

Throughout the evening Alex watched Bernie sizing up Ronnie. They went to the Fireside Inn, a pleasant steak house about halfway between Juliette and Lake George.

"So you're a cop," Bernie said after they'd given their order to the waiter.

Ronnie smiled. "Yes, I am. So you'd better behave yourself while you're on my turf."

Alex felt a surge of pride at how well she handled herself. Bernie could be intimidating. He was hard nosed, blunt to the point of rudeness, and he wasn't particularly worried about whether he hurt a person's feelings. Especially if he thought that person might be a threat to him or to one of his clients.

"So how'd you two meet?"

Alex fought to control his grin. Talk about obvious.

Ronnie chuckled. "Alex was speeding, and I stopped him and gave him a ticket."

"No kidding." Bernie removed a cigar from his lapel pocket.

"Mind if I smoke this?"

Ronnie shook her head. "No."

"I'm surprised he's still speakin' to you," Bernie added.

Now Alex gave vent to his amusement. "She gave me a pretty hard time," he admitted.

Ronnie's eyes sparkled, and she laughed, too. "He was obnoxious when I stopped him."

"Oh, come on," Alex said. "I wasn't that bad."

"Yes, you were."

"Well," Bernie said, "it doesn't seem to have made a difference. The two of you seem to be pretty good friends."

Oh, oh, thought Alex. Here it comes.

But Ronnie didn't get flustered by Bernie's obvious probing.

"We are," she said simply, giving Alex a warm smile—a smile that slid over him like thick honey. She really looked beautiful tonight. She was good-looking enough to give any woman a run for her money. Alex would have been proud to be seen with her anywhere.

The conversation remained casual while they ate their Caesar salads, a house specialty, and remained that way almost through the main course. Then, when Bernie had popped the last piece of his prime rib into his mouth and chewed lustily for a few minutes, he said, "How much work have you gotten done in the past eight weeks, Alex?"

"Act II is completely finished, and now I'm working on Act III."

"Havin' any problems with it?"

"Nothing I can't handle."

"I thought you'd of called me more often. I was getting worried."

Alex wouldn't have stood for that kind of questioning from many people, but Bernie had stood by him for a long time now, and Alex owed him something. So he counted to ten before answering. "No need to worry. Everything's going fine." Then before he thought, he said, "Ronnie's been helping me."

"And he's right, Mr. Maxwell. His work is wonderful."

"The name's Bernie," Bernie said as he relit his cigar and leaned back in his chair. "You know somethin' about writing then?"

"No, but—"

"She's been a great help to me," Alex interjected smoothly. Damn Bernie. He'd put up with a lot from him, but Bernie had no right to question Ronnie. "She's got good sense when it comes to plotting. She's already given me two or three great suggestions."

"Izzat so?" Bernie signalled for the waiter. "I'd like some coffee, and put a slug of brandy in it."

The waiter nodded. "Coffee for you, ma'am? You, sir? How about dessert? We make a really good German chocolate cake."

Alex and Ronnie gave him their orders, and the waiter left. By the time their dessert and coffee came, Alex managed to change the subject, and for the rest of the evening, Bernie regaled them with stories about the latest disasters on Broadway.

When they reached the house, Alex invited Ronnie in for a drink.

"No, I don't think so. Not tonight. You and Bernie probably have a lot to talk about, and you haven't had any time alone," she said.

He didn't push, because he knew Bernie was planning to go back to the city the next day, and they did have a lot to discuss. He took her hand and squeezed it. "See you tomorrow?"

"Sure." She smiled, then gently freed her hand and turned in the direction of her apartment.

Bernie was already pouring himself a snifter of brandy when Alex walked into the living room. "You want one?" he asked.

"Sure. Why not?" Alex sank onto the chintz-covered couch and stretched his legs out in front of him. He accepted the glass from Bernie and swirled the amber liquid around in the glass as he sniffed.

Bernie sat in one of the wing chairs. "So what's the story with the good-lookin' broad?"

Alex grinned. Good-looking broad. Wouldn't Ronnie bristle if she heard that description? "What do you mean?"

"Hey, kid, don't play dumb with me. I thought the whole idea of you comin' up here was to get away from the broads and all that. Now here I find you all cozied up to a pretty little girl, and it's obvious to me that you've been seein' a lot of her. So what gives?" Bernie took a sip of his brandy, then picked up his cigar and puffed.

The heavy sweetish smell of cigar smoke hung in the room. The question hung in the air.

Alex sighed. "Nothing *gives*, Bernie. Ronnie is a very attractive, very nice young woman, and we are friends. Nothing more."

"Yeah, and I'm probably gonna win the Mr. America contest next week." Bernie snorted.

Alex couldn't help smiling. Bernie, all five-feet-four of him, was at least thirty pounds overweight and balding, and he thought exercise was bending down to pick up the paper from his doorway each evening.

"You like this chick. I know you do." Bernie clamped his cigar between his teeth.

"Of course I like her. She's a terrific person. Hell, *you* liked her. I could tell." Alex sipped at his brandy, the fiery liquid warming his insides.

"Yeah . . . well, she's a foxy chick. Great ass."

"Bernie!" Alex laughed aloud.

"You didn't notice?" Bernie grinned.

"Oh, I noticed," Alex said.

"Thought so. So . . . you and her makin' it?"

"Now wait a minute," Alex said quickly. "That's none of your business!" He glared at the older man.

"Don't get your bowels in an uproar, kid. I've only got your best interests at heart. Remember what happens when you let your hormones control your life."

The conversation continued for a long time, and that night, as Alex lay in bed, he couldn't forget some of the things Bernie had said. Maybe it was a good thing Bernie had come this weekend. The situation with Ronnie had been nearing a crisis point, Alex knew that. And he also knew he'd be much better off if he didn't allow their relationship to go any further. Perhaps it would be best if he left Juliette very soon. The revisions to *Signposts* had gone very well so far—maybe he could finish them in the city. That's right, run away, he chided himself. Then, remembering that things always looked better in the light of day, he rolled over, punched up his pillow, and drifted off to sleep.

After church the next morning, Ronnie decided to do some work in the garden she and Sam shared. She put on an old pair of khaki shorts and a plain white

T-shirt and her beat-up Reeboks and socks. She put a white headband on to keep her curly hair out of her eyes and walked outside. The sun was already hot. It was going to be another scorcher, she thought. As she walked down her stairs, she saw the carriage house door open and Bernie Maxwell walk outside.

She grinned. He was dressed in blue plaid bermuda shorts and a dark blue golf shirt. He looked like a typical suburban husband off to play a round of golf on the weekend, instead of the hotshot New York agent she knew him to be.

As she neared the bottom of the steps, he turned and saw her. He raised his hand in greeting and walked toward her.

"Good morning," she said.

"Yeah, same to you. You gettin' ready to go runnin' or something?" He puffed on his cigar as his dark eyes studied her.

Ronnie shifted under his scrutiny. His eyes were more alive and aware than most people's, and she wondered why he made her feel so uneasy. "No," she said. "I was going to work in the garden for a while."

"How 'bout walkin' a bit with me?" he said.

Ronnie shrugged. "All right."

They started down the driveway and out onto the road. Mohawk Road was a narrow, two-lane street with wide dirt shoulders and not much traffic. They walked slowly along the shoulder of the road, and Ronnie wondered why he'd invited her to go along. She didn't have long to wait.

"Ronnie," he started. "You don't mind me callin' you Ronnie, do you?"

"No."

"I'm gonna say somethin' that I probably shouldn't. Alex would kill me if he knew I was sayin' it, but I'm gonna say it anyway."

Ronnie knew what was coming.

"You know how close me and Alex are?" he asked.

"Yes, I do."

"Yeah . . . well, I love the kid. I couldn't love him more if he was my own kid."

He sounded just like Sam, she thought.

"I want him to be happy, and I know bein' happy means bein' able to write. Alex is one of those rare people . . . people you and me can't ever be. He's got a monumental talent, Ronnie, and his writing is the most important thing in his life."

"I know that."

"Do you also know that Alex was almost destroyed by that bitch he married? She was an obsession with him, and when she left him, I really worried about his sanity." His voice had taken on a gruffness and an anger.

Ronnie shivered despite the heat of the sun beating down on them. "Why did she leave him?" she asked.

"Because she's selfish, spoiled, and immature. That's my opinion. 'Course, I can't ever say a word against her to Alex. He won't listen. I think he really thinks it's his fault they split. But the fact of the matter is, Margo didn't really want to be married. She wanted the bright lights and the fame, and she wanted to party every night and travel and spend money. She refused to face the plain fact that in order to have that money to do everything she loved doing, Alex had to write. And to write, he needed peace and serenity. Not parties and booze and stayin' up half the night."

"And that's why she left him?" Ronnie was incredulous.

"Yeah. Can you beat that? She couldn't stand the quiet life, and Alex couldn't live the way she wanted to, so one day she packed her bags and took off. And she broke his heart."

The woman must have been crazy, Ronnie thought. If she were married to Alex, she couldn't imagine leaving him for any reason, let alone one so shallow and unimportant.

"Anyway, Ronnie, Alex couldn't write for the whole year they were married, and then after she left, and he finally started to get over the whole thing, his writing was still missing the old magic. That's why I suggested he come up here. To get away from it all."

"And it's worked. Alex has read his work to me over the past few weeks, and it's wonderful."

"Yeah . . . maybe. But if he gets more involved with you, I'm afraid the same thing will happen as happened with Margo. This return of his ability to write seems fragile to me. I don't trust it yet." He stopped, shoved his hands in the pockets of his shorts and stared down the road. "Alex is very vulnerable right now," he said softly. He turned to look at her, his dark eyes bright and penetrating. "He doesn't need the complication of a woman in his life."

Ronnie looked down at her feet. Anything to evade

those knowing eyes. "We're just friends," she protested. "He says I've helped him." But her rejoinder sounded weak—even to her.

"Maybe so. But he's had a lot of unhappiness . . . a lot of rejection in his life . . . and he doesn't need anymore problems. I hope you understand that."

Ronnie knew she should be just as irritated with this funny little man as she had been with Sam and his unasked-for advice, but she wasn't. "I do," she said. "Don't worry. I wouldn't ever do anything to hurt Alex or hurt his writing. I admire and respect him and his work too much."

Bernie smiled. "Good. I knew you seemed like a sensible girl." His eyes twinkled. "Now how do you feel about an overweight, older man like me? I don't have any reason not to get involved with a great-lookin' broad like you. . . ."

SIX

Ronnie was still laughing when she and Bernie entered her yard. Bernie's blunt remark was uttered with such good humor and in such a teasing manner, she couldn't be offended.

"What's so funny?" said Alex from his doorway as they approached. "I hope you're not telling her stories about me."

"No. Nothing like that," Ronnie said between chuckles.

"You sure are conceited, thinking the only reason a beautiful girl could be laughing in my company is because we were talkin' about you," Bernie said.

"So where did you go?" Alex asked. His gray eyes roamed over Ronnie, and she felt a familiar stirring at the warmth in his gaze.

With a tiny catch in her voice, she said, "Just down the road . . . for a walk."

"Do you want to come in and have lunch with us? I'm fixing hamburgers. On the grill." Alex grinned, and Ronnie knew he was thinking the inducement of hamburgers would be all it took for her to accept the invitation. Ronnie loved hamburgers, and Alex knew it.

But she shook her head. "I don't think so. I promised Sam I'd work in the garden today. He was complaining the other day about having to do all the work this year, and I get half the proceeds."

"We're still on for dinner, aren't we?"

Why did he have to look at her like that? Ronnie could feel little chillbumps on her arms from the intensity of that smoky gaze. She glanced at Bernie Maxwell. His shrewd dark eyes stared steadily back. "Why don't we just skip tonight?" she said. "You probably want to spend time alone with Bernie."

"Bernie's leaving after lunch. Aren't you?" Alex said.

"Yeah. Gotta get back at a decent hour tonight," Bernie agreed.

"Well . . ." Ronnie said.

"It's settled, then. Come over here. I'll cook," Alex said with a satisfied smile. "Seven? Eight?"

"I'll come at eight." Then she turned to Bernie. "Since you're leaving soon, I'll say goodbye. I enjoyed meeting you, and I enjoyed our walk . . . and talk."

The evening air was thick with summer sounds and smells as Ronnie walked the short distance to the carriage house at eight o'clock that night. She could hear children laughing and splashing next door. The O'Hara children in their backyard pool, she thought. Sam's windows were all wide open. He refused to buy a window air conditioner, and Ronnie could hear the T.V. set blaring away. The carriage house didn't have an air conditioner either, so Ronnie had put on a lightweight red sundress and sandals.

At the door, she could hear the clear, lovely voice of Linda Ronstadt singing something old that Ronnie didn't recognize.

"I'm glad you're here," Alex said as he opened the door. "I've been working on Act III ever since Bernie left, and I've got a problem I can't figure out how to solve. I want to read it to you." He ran his fingers through his dark hair. He grabbed her hands and pulled her inside.

Ronnie allowed him to lead her into the living room, and she could see he wasn't kidding when he said he'd been working. Papers littered the room, and the typewriter still sat on the desk in front of the window.

Alex poured her a glass of white wine without asking her if she wanted it, and after he handed it to her, she sat on one end of the couch and sipped while Alex sat on the other end of the couch and read the part bothering him. "What do you think?" he asked when he finished.

"I think it's wonderful," she said. "I don't quite understand what . . ."

Alex jumped up and began to pace. As he talked, he punctuated his sentences by jabbing his finger in her direction. His gray eyes blazed. Ronnie couldn't help thinking that even in his agitation, he looked wonderful in his white shorts and open-weave white shirt. She could see all the muscles in his legs and arms and chest ripple as he walked rapidly back and forth. Her chest tightened, and her pulse accelerated. He exuded pure animal magnetism, and Ronnie didn't know how much longer she'd be able to spend so much time in his company without going crazy from frustration.

". . . So you see," Alex finished. "Jack looks like a fool when he turns down Maria's offer, and I don't know how to make him look sympathetic. I don't want the audience to laugh at him. I want them to feel his pain and realize what it's cost him to say 'no' to her."

Ronnie tried to ignore her strong awareness of him as she concentrated on the problem Alex had presented. Finally, in a hesitant voice, she said, "I . . . I could be wrong. I'm not creative, like you are, but I really think the problem is you haven't shown me Jack's motivation for his actions. That's why I can't feel the sympathy you're looking for. I don't know *why* he's turning Maria down."

Alex's mouth dropped open. He stared at her. Then he threw his head back and shouted. "Good Lord! You're absolutely right! I can't believe it!" He took two long strides, grabbed her hands, and pulled her up. He put his arms around her and hugged her, lifting her up off her feet in his exuberance.

Ronnie could feel every taut muscle in his chest and smell the unique male smell he exuded, mixed in with his spicy sandalwood cologne. She closed her eyes and revelled in the heady sensation his nearness caused. Still keeping her in the circle of his arms, he let her body slide down his until she was once again on her feet. The friction caused by the contact of her body moving against his made Ronnie feel so weak, she could hardly stand up. A tremor shook her body, and Alex's strong arms tightened.

On the stereo Linda crooned about moon and June, and Alex said huskily, "Veronica?"

Ronnie looked up. His eyes were twin magnets of smoky gray. She could see flecks of black in their depths, and as she watched, his eyes changed and softened, became cloudy with warmth and desire. Incapable of speech, she clung to him, her heart hammering against her chest erratically as she watched his face descend.

At the first touch of his warm lips, Ronnie felt as if someone had set off a firecracker in her body. An explosion of feeling consumed her—a dizzying mixture of happiness and love and an aching need and the overpowering urge to give. Oh, Alex, her mind cried. *Oh, Alex.*

"Oh, God," he moaned against her open mouth. Ronnie felt as if she were melting, as if she had no bones. His warm, slightly rough palms massaged her bare back, stroked her arms, caressed the back of her neck, and his demanding mouth claimed hers again and again.

Ronnie whimpered as his hands found her breasts. An unbearable longing shot through her, centering itself in her throbbing core. Love me, love me, she prayed.

"Oh, God, Ronnie. I want you," Alex whispered raggedly as his hands lifted her skirt. He slowly stroked her bare legs. The heat from his hands burned her skin.

"Yes," she murmured. "Yes."

Without another word, Alex put his hands underneath her and lifted her off her feet. Before Ronnie could catch her breath, he shouldered his way into the bedroom and gently laid her on the big double bed. The last bit of twilight gave the room a soft, lavender glow. Ronnie could hear the song of crickets outside the open window and the accompanying song of Linda on the stereo. She could feel the slightly rough chenille bedspread under her sensitized skin. She waited.

Alex sat beside her. In the pale light, she could see his eyes gleaming and his chest moving rapidly up and down. She could hear his still uneven breathing and see the evidence of his passion and desire. With his fingertips, he traced the outline of her collarbone, then dropped his fingers to the hollow between her breasts. Slowly, he leaned over her and placed his moist mouth where his fingertips had been. Ronnie's heart leapt, and the sweet pain of longing burst within her.

"Are you sure?" he whispered against her skin. His breath sent a shiver along her body.

"Yes," she said. She touched his hair as he kissed the delicate skin on top of her breasts. His hair felt thick and silky, just the way she'd known it would. "Yes."

Alex raised himself up. Then very gently, he pulled her into a sitting position. With trembling fingers, he untied the straps of her sundress. As he pulled the top down, Ronnie's bare breasts were exposed, and she shivered as he touched first one, then the other.

When he bent to kiss them, she closed her eyes, savoring each stabbing, exquisitely tormenting sensation.

Alex slowly removed her dress and then, almost reverently, her lacy underpants. As his warm hands slid under their elastic tops and pulled them down, Ronnie's breath caught. His fingers stroked her gently as he watched her face. "Do you like that?" he whispered.

"Oh, yes," she said. You could do anything, she thought. Anything. And I'd love it. Because I love you.

"Veronica?"

"Yes?"

Alex pulled his shirt over his head, then tugged his shorts off. "Are you on the pill?"

Her eyes widened. "No."

"Are you protected at all?"

Very little light was left in the room, but Ronnie heard the gruffness, the concern in his voice. "No," she admitted.

"I'll take care of it, then," he said. He leaned over her, kissed her hard and muttered, "Don't go away."

As if I could, she thought. Nothing could drag me away. Not now.

When Alex returned to the bedroom, he lowered himself next to Ronnie, turned her to face him, and caressed her with a sure, yet gentle touch. Each loving stroke added to the steadily building heat in Ronnie's body. She closed her eyes and gave herself up to the feelings his hands and lips elicited. She shuddered as his hot mouth found her sensitive places; she throbbed with a torture both agonizing and sweet. She could feel his growing need, and as she tentatively reached for him and touched him gently, he stiffened and gasped.

"Veronica . . ." His hands grasped her, pulled her tight against him, and his mouth covered hers, demanding, scalding, claiming her for his own.

Ronnie's heart thundered in her ears. A great rush of desire consumed her, and at her eager response Alex moaned softly.

When he lifted himself over her and joined their two bodies, Ronnie gasped. At first she felt pain, but soon she answered his movements with movements of her own, and Ronnie felt that kindling sensation again, as if he were slowly adding bits of fuel to the fire in her body. Soon the heat consumed her until her very center ignited, sending flames and sparks to each nerve ending of her body in one great rush of blazing glory.

As shudders shook Ronnie's body, Alex lost control, and soon his own cries joined hers as pleasure spiraled through him. His arms tightened around her, and he could feel her heartbeat against him. Keeping their two bodies locked together, he gently rolled onto his back, holding her clasped against him. He loved the feel of her moist, warm skin against his length; he loved being inside her. He buried his face in her silky, fragrant hair, breathing in its lemony fragrance.

God, she was sweet. He closed his eyes and listened to the muted sounds of the evening. He felt enclosed in a safe, warm world where nothing from the outside could ever touch him or Ronnie. A sense of well-being and something else, something hard to define, seemed to permeate his body. And it was more than the ordinary afterglow of good sex. This was more like the feeling of coming home after being away a very long time. This was a feeling of rightness, a desire to keep Ronnie here, next to him, always. As if this were where she belonged.

His hand caressed her hair, then her cheek. Her breathing had slowed, and he could feel her feathery breath on his chest. He stroked the strong, smooth muscles of her back, then the sweet, round contours of her bottom. Ronnie trembled against him.

"Oh, Alex . . ." she murmured. "I . . . I never thought I could feel this way . . . that it could be like this," she said softly.

His arms tightened. "You're wonderful," he whispered.

Her hands played with the hair on his chest, and Alex could feel himself responding, growing harder inside her.

Alex's grip on her tightened, and he began to move his hips against hers. She lifted her head, and he pulled her head against his, kissing her with an almost savage intensity. Soon the flames began to grow once more, leaping and building until he and Ronnie were spun into the vortex of fiery passion once more.

Later, as they lay beside each other, sated and exhausted, Alex kissed her gently. His hand cupped one small, perfect breast, stroking its smooth, soft skin. He could feel her heart beating against his palm. Outside, the muted sound of a car passing on the road beyond and the steady singing of crickets seemed to echo his own jumbled feelings as they whirled in his mind, a mixture of happiness and guilt. Guilt because she'd given so generously without asking for anything in return. He pulled her against him, tucked her head under his chin and closed his eyes. "Oh, Ronnie," he said. "I hope you're not sorry."

"Sorry?" Her arms tightened. "Don't be silly. I'm happier than I've ever been. It . . . it was absolutely wonderful, and I loved it, and I'm not sorry in the least." Then she chuckled—a soft, endearing sound. "I'm only sorry we wasted so much time."

He smiled. She was enchanting, this little dynamo who had somehow wormed her way into the recesses of his heart—a place he'd never intended to let anyone occupy again. "Well, we've still got a lot of time left," he said. His hand moved in lazy circles against her back. "Including a very long night."

The next morning, Alex awakened at the first faint pinkness of dawn. A lone bird twittered and chirped outside the bedroom window, and a soft breeze lifted the gauzy curtains and rattled the blind. Ronnie stirred, but soon settled back into sleep. Alex propped himself on his arm and looked at her. Her soft lips were slightly open, and he could just see the tip of her small, pink tongue. Her dark lashes rested against smooth cheeks, and her thick, curly hair lay in dark, moist tendrils around her face.

They had eventually banished the chenille bedspread to the floor last night and now lay on the blue and white flowered sheets. Sometime during the night, one of them had pulled the top sheet up over them, because Ronnie's body was concealed from the waist down, but Alex could see her lovely breasts—the skin whiter than the skin of her neck and shoulders. Her hip jutted in a tantalizing curve from her narrow waist, then sloped downward again as it blended in with her shapely thighs and legs.

As Alex watched her sleep, he could feel his body once again stirring with desire. She was amazing, he thought. Completely captivating and capable of bringing him to the point of total surrender. Why did he feel this overpowering need for her? What was it about her that had melted every defense he'd built, every barrier he'd thought existed between him and his ability to feel this way again? Again? Be honest, he told himself. You've never felt this way before. You were obsessed with Margo, true, but you never felt this protectiveness, the total sharing and understanding you felt with Ronnie last night.

He wanted to reach out and touch her, kiss her into wakefulness. He wanted to see those blue, blue eyes looking at him as he brought her body to the peak again. He wanted to watch each reaction, store it in his mind to be savored over and over again.

But he held back, because mixed with the swelling feelings of desire were the tricklings of uneasiness. Hadn't he always known Ronnie wouldn't give herself lightly? So what did this mean? Did she think, hope, that their becoming lovers would mean a more permanent commitment? Alex's stomach muscles tightened. He'd decided after the fiasco with Margo that he'd never marry again. In his gut he felt marriage wasn't for him. Now he wondered if he'd inadvertently led Ronnie to believe otherwise. He rolled over onto his back, clenching his fists in frustration. God, he hoped he hadn't misled her. She was too fine a person for him to play with her emotions. Filled with conflicting feelings, Alex rolled onto his side, away from Ronnie, and fell into a fitful sleep.

Ronnie opened her eyes. Bright sunshine filled the room, and the air felt warm with the promise of a hot day. Birds chirped outside her window, and she could hear the O'Hara children laughing and shouting. A cat meowed, and Ronnie turned to look out the window and saw Alex's back.

Remembrances of last night flooded her mind and filled her body with tingling awareness. Alex. She smiled, stretched, and rolled toward him, putting her lips against the smooth contours of his muscled back. She kissed him with light, nipping kisses and slid her arm around him, stroking his chest and pulling herself against him as she touched him. She felt him come awake, felt the tightening of his muscles.

She sat up and bent over him, kissing his ear and murmuring playfully, "Wake up, lazybones. We're wasting a perfectly good day by lying in bed. Besides, I've got to get to work. What time is it, anyway?" Then she spied the clock on his dresser. "Good grief! It's eight!"

Alex sat up. "I forgot to set the alarm." He looked at her, his gray eyes filled with warmth.

Ronnie loved the way his hair fell into his eyes, the way his face was still flushed with sleep. She wished she could call in sick. "I've got to get home, but I'd better call in and say I'll be late," she said regretfully.

Alex got up and padded toward the bathroom, calling over his shoulder, "Go ahead. In the meantime, I'll get dressed."

"I wish you didn't have to," Ronnie said softly, but he had already closed the bathroom door. She would have liked to look at his body in the light of day. Last night she'd been too shy to really look, and the light had faded fast. She wished she could stop to examine her feelings. She wished they could make love again. She wished she could stay.

Sighing, she got out of bed, collected her clothes from the floor, and hurriedly dressed. She walked over to Alex's dresser and picked up his hairbrush, giving her hair a couple of swipes. Then she stopped and looked at herself in the mirror. Her eyes had a slumberous look, and her lips looked swollen. Her skin glowed. Why, anyone who looks at me can tell what I've been doing, she thought. Then she smiled. And I don't even care.

The bathroom door opened, and Alex emerged in a white, terrycloth bathrobe. His gray eyes studied her gravely. Then he walked over and put his hands on her shoulders. He bent down and kissed her softly. "Veronica, there's something I have to say."

She opened her mouth, and he kissed her again. "No. Be quiet. Let me talk."

Please don't apologize, she prayed. Please don't.

"I have to say this," he said, his voice gruff. "I know you told me you're not sorry, but I can't help feeling a little guilty about what's happened."

"I . . . I don't understand why you should feel guilty," she said softly. "I'm a grownup. I made my own choice. You didn't force me."

His hands tightened on her shoulders. "I know that, but I also know what sort of person you are, and I can't make you any promises. I . . . I wish I could, but I can't."

"I know," she whispered. "I always knew that. That's not why we made love, is it? We made love because we wanted each other, we wanted to give each other something, and there's really no need for promises, is there?"

She saw uncertainty flicker in his eyes, then his hands relaxed their grip, and he pulled her against his chest. She could hear his heartbeat echo her own, and she closed her eyes and breathed in the earthy, male smell of him. "I don't want promises from you, Alex."

"Are you sure?" His voice rumbled against her hair.

"I'm sure. Let's just enjoy what we have . . . what we've found together . . . and not worry about the future."

Then his mouth found hers in a deep, drugging kiss, and Ronnie really believed what she'd said. This moment was enough. If this moment were all she ever had, it would be enough.

SEVEN

If the beginning of the summer had seemed like a golden, magical time to Ronnie, the last half of the summer, after she and Alex became lovers, seemed like a fiery, blazing interlude of passion and desire. Each sense fully awakened. The sun shone brighter and hotter, the sky shimmered with a more intense blue than ever before, the leaves glistened in emerald splendor, the vibrant pinks and scarlets of the roses deepened, the song of the birds harmonized with silver clarity, and Ronnie's own body existed in a tremor of constant arousal and heightened awareness.

All Alex had to do was turn that melting gray gaze her way, and Ronnie could feel herself tingle. Her skin seemed more sensitive, and even the lightest cloth rubbing against it could produce that breath-catching expectancy and need.

She couldn't believe how wonderful she felt. She was afraid everyone who looked at her would know what was happening in her life. She avoided Sam as much as possible, terrified he'd take one look at her face and eyes and body and instantly know how completely committed to Alex she was, how he'd invaded her mind and skin and soul.

Ronnie didn't kid herself. She loved the sex, but she also knew she loved Alex—loved him with everything she had in her—loved him so completely she couldn't imagine how she'd ever existed in a world without him. Or how she'd go on with her life once he left Juliette.

But she closed off that part of her mind. She tried not to think about how devastated she'd be when he was gone. She pretended; pretended everything was the same as it had always been, that the only thing different about her was that she finally understood what being a woman was all about.

But down deep, down in the recesses of her heart, she knew nothing was the same. Or ever would be. Alex Summerfield had come into her life and taken her heart, and that heart would always belong to him. He'd also taken her body, and her body would bear his imprint forever. It would ache for him when he was gone, and no one else could ever make it feel quite the same way he had.

So she moved through the days of July and early August in a world where reality was Alex and his smile, his rich voice, his smoky eyes, his kisses and his hands and his touches—touches that brought her to those shattering peaks of pleasure that seemed to be all she thought about.

Ronnie had never considered herself sensuous. The realization that Alex had unearthed the hidden Ronnie, and the discovery that she had responses and desires never before awakened both surprised and shook her. To someone who had always been in control of her life, this sudden loss of control, this sudden dependence on another person, was almost frightening. But like a starving person to a banquet, she was inexorably drawn to Alex.

People noticed the change in her. One morning Maisie said, "You sure are lookin' good, sheriff."

"Why, thanks," said Ronnie. She smiled, thinking of the way Alex had looked at her when she'd left his bed only an hour earlier.

"Who's the guy?"

"What . . . ?" Ronnie's head jerked around, and she stopped in front of Maisie's desk.

Maisie grinned and blew an enormous bubble, then popped it. Her red hair bobbed up and down as her head moved. "You heard me," she said with a mischievous twinkle in her green eyes. "There's got to be a guy. A woman doesn't have the kind of glow you've got if she's spendin' her nights with a good book!"

Ronnie could feel her face heating up.

Maisie giggled, but before she could make another comment, the telephone buzzed, and she turned her attention to the caller. Ronnie took the opportunity to escape to her office, but Maisie's comment gave her something to think about.

Only a few days later, Joyce MacAllister, a new deputy, stuck her head around the doorway of Ronnie's office and said, "Hey, Ronnie . . . uh, I mean, sheriff . . ."

Ronnie looked up from the deposition she was

reading. "It's all right to call me Ronnie when no one else is around, Joyce."

"Well . . . uh . . . a bunch of us are going over to Saratoga tonight. Would you like to go with us?" Joyce pushed a strand of blonde hair back and repinned it. Her hair was very long, but she refused to cut it. Instead she twisted it into a thick chignon and kept it confined with pins. The department had a rule about hair. Anything above the shoulder could be worn loose. Anything that hung below the shoulder had to be pinned up.

"Thanks, Joyce. I appreciate the invitation, but I'm busy tonight."

Joyce grinned, then astounded Ronnie by winking. "I was hoping maybe the two of you were no longer seeing each other," she said. "Give the rest of us a chance."

Ronnie could feel that damned blush invading her face again. "I have no idea what you're talking about," she said, but she ducked her head, avoiding Joyce's eyes and pretending not to hear the knowing laugh as Joyce walked away.

That night she told Alex about the two episodes, adding laughingly, "See what you've done? I have no secrets anymore. Everyone in the office is probably talking about me behind my back. And this is too small a town for them not to realize who the man is!" She punched him, and he grabbed her. The two of them wrestled for a few minutes, finally falling on the floor like two children.

Soon the playful touches changed, became intimate, sensual, heated. Alex saw Ronnie's eyes grow heavy with desire as his hands roamed demandingly over her responsive body. He forgot everything then—everything except this vibrant woman in his arms. But later, as they lay quietly, side by side, he thought about her telling remark.

What am I doing to her? he wondered. Was it fair for him to monopolize her this way, to keep taking and taking without giving her anything in return? He knew his behavior was weak and selfish, he knew he was taking advantage of her generosity and sweetness, but he couldn't bring himself to put an end to their love affair. Dozens of times over the past weeks he'd told himself he'd pack up and leave, get away from Ronnie and the temptation to keep taking what she offered, but each time they were together his resolve would crumble. His need for her would override both his good sense and his promises to himself.

Looking at her now, he felt his heart squeeze painfully in his chest. She was so beautiful. Her face, flushed from their lovemaking; her mouth, swollen from his kisses; her eyes, hooded and heavy; her body, silky and smooth. How could he bear to leave her? How could he stay?

He knew he had to take some kind of action . . . and soon. The situation couldn't go on like this forever. In less than three weeks he was scheduled to leave Juliette and go back to New York City.

Alex buried his face in her sweet-smelling hair and held her close. He didn't want to think about anything tonight. All he wanted was Ronnie, here, in his arms. Tomorrow was soon enough for decisions.

* * *

Ronnie rubbed her eyes with the back of her hand. God, she felt tired today. She smiled to herself. Well, was it any wonder she was tired? Alex had seemed almost insatiable the night before. But Ronnie thought she understood his need. He would be leaving soon, and she knew he felt some of the same desperation she felt when she allowed herself to think about the future.

Her intercom buzzed, jolting her out of her semi-daydream.

"Sheriff? It's Miss Agatha on line one," said Maisie.

Ronnie picked up the phone. "Hello? Miss Agatha?"

"Hello, Veronica," said Miss Agatha in her precise voice. "I haven't seen you for a while."

"I'm sorry, Miss Agatha. I've been so busy."

"Doing what?"

Ronnie smiled. Miss Agatha wouldn't consider her question an invasion of Ronnie's privacy. "Oh, this and that. You know . . ."

"No, I do not. Otherwise I wouldn't have asked."

Struggling to keep the chuckle out of her voice, Ronnie tapped her pencil against the smooth metal desktop and said, "Jogging, gardening, swimming, dating . . . you know . . . normal things."

"I hope you're not too busy to keep an eye on that scoundrel, Alex Summerfield."

Ronnie laughed.

"You may laugh, my dear, but I assure you, this is no laughing matter," said Miss Agatha crisply. "This is a serious affair."

Oh, you bet it is! Ronnie thought. "In what way?" she asked seriously.

Miss Agatha dropped her voice to a conspiratorial whisper. "I think Mr. Summerfield is here to spy on us."

Ronnie's mouth dropped open.

"Well? Say something," Miss Agatha ordered.

"I . . . I can't think what to say," Ronnie said honestly. Was Miss Agatha's mental health impaired? Ronnie had always thought the old lady to be astute and sharp, but perhaps old age had caught up with her. Maybe she'd become senile. "Wh . . . what makes you think Alex Summerfield is a spy?" she finally said.

"Because he acts suspiciously!"

Ronnie frowned. "How so?"

"Well," Miss Agatha said slowly, "yesterday I caught him peeking in my kitchen window!"

Ronnie laughed at the absurd picture of a stealthy Alex peering through Miss Agatha's window.

"You may laugh, young lady, but I found his behavior quite odd!"

"Yes, I can see how you might." Ronnie smothered another chuckle, then in her best "sheriff" voice said, "And what did you say to him?"

"Veronica," Miss Agatha said haughtily, "when you are trying to determine what someone is doing, you do not *say* anything. You merely watch. And wait."

"I see," Ronnie murmured. Curiouser and curiouser, she thought. "Well? What happened?"

"After he stopped looking into my window like a

common Peeping Tom, I opened my back door and told him to come in."

"Told him to come in . . ." Ronnie echoed.

"Veronica, if you insist on repeating every single word I utter, we will never get anywhere."

Ronnie choked. "I'm sorry, Miss Agatha," she apologized. "It's just that what you say is so hard for me to believe."

"Hummph! You act as if I'm making this up. I seem to remember another time you scoffed at me, and look what happened then!"

Darn Alex. If he hadn't lifted that Hummel, Miss Agatha wouldn't have a leg to stand on, Ronnie thought.

". . . So just trust me when I tell you that man is up to no good, and I think you should watch him closely!"

It took Ronnie ten more minutes to soothe Miss Agatha's ruffled feathers, and in the end, Ronnie promised the older woman she'd do her best to keep Alex under her watchful eye.

Later that day, after Ronnie had cooked hamburgers for herself and Alex, and they were sitting side by side on the glider on his back patio, she said, "I had a really strange phone call from Miss Agatha today." She sighed contentedly as she rested her head on his shoulder.

"And what did Miss Agatha have to say that was so strange?" he asked, nuzzling the top of her head.

Ronnie told him, and he laughed aloud.

"I think she's lost her sanity, Alex. I'm worried

about her. Maybe I should talk to Hannah about getting Miss Agatha to see a doctor."

"That old lady is shrewder and more sane than either you or I," Alex said between chuckles. "No. She's got some reason for this cat and mouse game she's playing with us. In fact, I think I have an idea what she's up to."

"You do? What?"

"I'd rather not say until I'm sure."

"Come on, Alex. What?"

"I'm not going to tell you until I'm sure. Believe me, sooner or later the reason will become apparent. Then I'll know if I'm right or wrong."

"I hope you're right. I really like Miss Agatha. I'd hate to think she's getting senile."

"I'm right."

"Do you really think so?"

"Trust me," Alex said. "We'll find out what she's up to. I guarantee it."

"And in the meantime?"

"In the meantime we'll just sit and wait. But you *can* keep a close eye on me. I don't mind." His voice had dropped to a suggestive whisper, and his hand stole around the front of her.

As Alex's insistent hands began to work their magic, Ronnie closed her eyes. A delicious weakness overcame her, and her breathing became shallow. "Oh, Alex," she whispered. "You're like a drug . . . the way you make me feel."

"Let's go inside," he whispered. "You can watch me even closer inside."

Shaking with laughter and anticipation, Ronnie stood

up, and hand in hand they walked inside, shutting the door on the world.

On a steamy August afternoon several days later, Ronnie pulled into her driveway at the end of the day and spotted Alex sitting on her bottom step, legs sprawled out in front of him and a silly grin on his face.

She grinned back, a good feeling of warmth slowly spreading through her body. "Hi," she said.

"Hi," he said. He stood up and stretched.

Ronnie's heart did a lazy somersault as she watched his taut muscles ripple against the thin fabric of his clinging red T-shirt. Sweat glistened on his arms and legs and darkened the front of his shirt.

"I was waiting for you," he said, his gray eyes as fathomless as a dark sea.

"So I see." Her voice caught in her throat. She had an overwhelming desire to throw herself into his arms—to feel the heat of his body against hers—to make love with him here, now, in the hot sun, lying on the grass with the earth beneath them. The force of her desire stunned her.

As if he knew her thoughts, could see right down inside her, his tongue moved slowly over his lower lip, and his eyes held hers locked in a tight gaze. "I've been thinking about you all day," he said.

Ronnie dragged in a shaky breath. Her knees turned to pudding, and her heart thudded madly against her rib cage. Wordlessly, she reached for his hand, the feel of his warm palm sending slivers of desire into every corner of her body.

"Come upstairs," she whispered.

She had to release his hand to open her door, but the minute he kicked the door shut behind him, he reached for her, pulling her roughly into his arms. His hungry mouth claimed hers, and Ronnie's head spun dizzily as his tongue plunged deep into her mouth again and again.

"I need you," he muttered, his breath ragged.

I need you, too, she thought. More every day. Desperately and incessantly.

His hands pulled at her uniform, and in his haste, a button skittered to the floor. Then his hands and hot mouth found her breasts, and Ronnie shivered and moaned at the barrage of sweet torture.

She never knew how they managed to rid each other of the rest of their encumbering clothes—their mutual need driving every other thought from her mind.

Together they tumbled to the floor, and there, in the sultry heat of the August day, in the middle of Ronnie's kitchen floor, with the late afternoon sun pouring through her windows in fiery brilliance, they greedily came together in a torrid, all-consuming union of sizzling urgency and wild abandon.

As shudders of ecstasy radiated through her quivering body, Ronnie gripped Alex's sweat-slick shoulders and knew there was no other person in the world who could ever bring her to this place of blazing splendor or ever make her feel like this except this man . . . the man she loved. Only you, she thought. Forever. I'll belong to you forever.

"Ronnie, sweet Ronnie," Alex murmured as he

gently feathered kisses on her face and neck. Their mutual need had been sated, and Ronnie lay with her head cradled on Alex's shoulder, basking in the golden glow of glory that always followed their lovemaking. "I . . . I didn't mean to attack you like that," he continued softly. "I didn't hurt you, did I?" His fingers touched her breasts, and Ronnie smiled.

"Hurt me? I loved it, Alex. Couldn't you tell?" She clasped his hand against her breast to still his teasing touch. "Don't you know that sometimes a woman wants to be taken like that? Wants to feel she's needed desperately—that her man can't wait—can't be gentle because he needs her too much?"

"You know, I never intended to need anyone again," he said gruffly.

Ronnie held her breath. Was he finally going to tell her about Margo?

"I thought . . . after my marriage broke up . . . when I was so unhappy . . . that I never wanted to feel that way again."

"Tell me about it," Ronnie said softly.

He sighed deeply and stroked Ronnie's hair. "Have you ever felt like everyone else in the world knows a secret you don't know?"

"Yes." She'd felt that way about love until she'd met Alex, but she didn't say it.

"Well, it seems to me now that I always felt that way. From the day my parents died and I went to live with my aunt Isabel, I felt like all the other people in the world knew what life was all about, but I was just a spectator. I always felt this void. Now, of course, I realize I just felt as if no one loved me. Then I met Margo."

His voice changed when he said her name, and Ronnie's chest felt tight. Did he still love her?

"She was like a fresh breeze in a room filled with cigar smoke. She had a laugh like tinkling bells, and she was breathtaking . . . gorgeous . . . everyone loved her. People swarmed around her like honeybees around a rich, beautiful flower.

"I was just as bad as the rest of them. I couldn't take my eyes off her. She seemed like sunshine in a dark room. When she noticed me, when she acted as if she liked me, I floated around on clouds. I didn't come down to earth again for a long, long time. . . ."

Ronnie knew how he had felt. She'd been floating around on that same cloud for weeks now.

"We were married two weeks after we met," he continued. "My delirium lasted six months." His voice was now dry and emotionless, and he rapidly related the rest of his story. "And that's what it was—delirium. We partied and stayed up until the wee hours every night and made love and ate too much and drank too much and generally led a life of the pursuit of pleasure and little else.

"When I got tired of it all and tried to settle back to a normal routine . . . to writing . . . Margo would pout and tease and wheedle until I'd do whatever it was she wanted. When I refused, she'd go without me. Then I started hearing rumors about her and another man. I couldn't stand it. I wanted to kill her.

"One night after we'd been married about a year, we had a terrible fight. We shouted at each other, and she threw something at me, and I grabbed her . . . and nearly hit her. The shock of realizing how close I'd come to violence really threw me. It was only then I realized how low I'd sunk . . . how bad for me our relationship was.

"She left the next day. She packed up everything and went off to Europe. That was over two years ago, and the only word I've had from her has been through her lawyer."

He's never forgotten her, Ronnie thought. Her arms tightened around him.

"My ego must have been very fragile," he said. "Intellectually I knew I hadn't done anything wrong, but emotionally I felt as if there was something lacking in me if I couldn't keep my own wife happy. It's taken me a long time to realize that neither of us were at fault. We simply didn't belong together. We hadn't taken any time to get to know each other. We were blinded by our strong sexual attraction and obsession, and we let ourselves think it was love.

"I . . . I'm not sure I ever really loved Margo," he said. "But I did need her desperately, and I was crushed when she left me. I hadn't done any writing while we were married, and after she was gone, I still couldn't write . . . not for a long time. The loss of the ability to write was worse in its way than the loss of Margo. I felt completely alone . . . completely abandoned.

"It took almost a whole year before I began to write again, and even then, the writing was missing something. It wasn't until I came up here that I really recovered. It's been a long, difficult fight to regain peace of mind and the confidence to be able to write well again.''

Ronnie sighed. "Thank you for telling me, Alex. I've wondered, of course."

"I vowed I'd never let myself need anyone like that again." His voice softened, and he turned her face so that he could look into her eyes. "But I hadn't counted on meeting you, sheriff. You've managed to disrupt every plan and shatter every promise I made. I'm still trying to figure out how you did it."

Even as he said it, Alex knew that wasn't what he was trying to decide. He knew how she'd done it. She'd done it by being the person she was—sweet and giving, passionate and loving, vulnerable and strong, charming and funny. His Veronica. The only unanswered question was what he was going to do now.

EIGHT

It was the beginning of the last week of August, and Alex would be leaving in eight days. Eight days. The words drummed in Ronnie's mind like a tom tom. Eight days. I won't think about it, she told herself over and over again, but like a burglar creeping soundlessly in the night, the knowledge peeked around corners, catching her off-guard and vulnerable, so that a sudden, sharp pain would catch at her heart, and the words would beat relentlessly in her mind. Eight days. Only eight days. Then he'll be gone. Oh, God. How can I stand it? She squeezed her eyes tight, and the hot tears that had threatened to spill over were forced back.

"Ronnie? Are you all right?"

Ronnie blinked. Maisie stood in the open doorway, a quizzical look on her narrow, freckled face.

"I was just coming back from the restroom when I saw you, and you looked like something was hurting you," Maisie explained in a rush.

Ronnie frowned. "I'm all right. Just a headache."

"Better take something."

"I will." Why didn't Maisie go away?

Finally she did, and Ronnie forced herself to push all thoughts of Alex out of her mind.

At three thirty that afternoon, Maisie buzzed her on the intercom and said, "Elmira Crutchins just called, Ronnie." Her voice rose in excitement. "She said you'd better hurry over to the Jacobsens' house because Pete is at it again . . . and this time it sounds real bad!"

Ronnie jumped up, grabbed her holster and revolver, jammed her hat on her head and raced out her door. "Come with me!" she called to William. "I might need help."

Ten minutes later, as they careened into the Jacobsens' yard, Ronnie prayed that Laurie Jacobsen would be all right. She and William raced up the sagging porch steps, and William banged on the screen door. An ominous quiet answered their knocks.

"Pete! Laurie!" Ronnie shouted. She and William looked at each other as the quiet persisted. William pulled at the door, but it was hooked from the inside.

"Cut the screen," Ronnie said and watched as William pulled out his pocket knife and quickly slit the screen around the perimeter. Then he reached inside and unlatched the door. He opened the door, and Ronnie walked into the hot, dark house. The stale odor of onions and grease hung heavily in the air, and she wrinkled her nose.

"Laurie?" Ronnie called again.

Ronnie heard the sound of a door slamming, and she darted into the kitchen. Then she saw them.

Laurie lay on the kitchen floor next to one of her little boys. Her wispy brown hair was clotted with blood, and she had a mottled, purple bruise on her right cheek. The boy had an angry red welt on his forehead and a cut on his upper lip. Laurie's mouth was puffed up, and blood oozed from a cut under her left eye. Her eyes were closed, and Ronnie dropped to her knees. She lowered her head to Laurie's chest and listened.

"She's breathing," Ronnie said. She lifted Laurie's limp wrist, felt its clamminess, and put her fingers over the weak pulse. "I can still feel it," she told William, who was lifting the boy.

"He seems all right; his eyes are open now," William said.

"Where's the other boy, I wonder?" Ronnie said. "Go lay him on the couch in the front room; see if you can find the other boy."

While William followed her orders, Ronnie wet a washcloth and squeezed it out, laying it on Laurie's forehead. Then she straightened up and looked for the telephone. She spied it on the wall, but when she lifted the receiver, the line was dead. Probably didn't pay their bill, she thought. She walked out to the living room, and through the screen door she could see Elmira Crutchins standing on the porch.

Ronnie opened the door and shouted, "Elmira, call the hospital and ask them to send an ambulance, will you? Laurie's hurt, and so is one of the boys."

Elmira nodded, and without a word, she spun around. Her fat legs carried her faster than Ronnie would have thought possible.

As Ronnie turned around, William came down the hall from the bedrooms with the other little boy in his arms. The child hid his face against William's chest.

"He's okay. He was hiding in the closet," William explained.

When the ambulance arrived, Ronnie stepped back and allowed the attendants to take charge. One of them, a tall, dark-haired young man, said, "The kids are okay. All they really need is some aspirin and rest, but the woman needs a doctor's attention."

"Take her," Ronnie ordered. "I'll take care of the kids." She made a quick decision. "Load the kids in the car, William. We'll take them with us." That way, she thought, if Pete should come back, he couldn't vent his anger on them again.

"Where are we taking them, sheriff?" asked William as they headed back toward the center of town.

"To my house."

"Your house?"

She heard the incredulity in his voice. "Oh, I'm not going to keep them myself. I'm going to ask Sam to keep them temporarily."

"Do you think he will?"

"I'm positive he will," Ronnie said. Inwardly, she wondered if she were right. Maybe Sam would be so bent out of shape at her neglect of him, he'd refuse to help her.

But he didn't disappoint her. His dark eyes clouded with concern as Ronnie explained what had happened.

"Poor little tykes," he said. "Of course they can stay with me." He turned to the boy who had been hiding in the closet and patted the pale blond head. "Do you like to watch T.V.?"

Ronnie grinned as she saw the almost instant empathy and understanding pass between the two. The kids would be all right, she thought. "Thanks, Sam," she said softly.

He put his arm around her shoulder. "How are you doin?"

"I'm just fine."

"You look terrific."

"Thanks."

"Ronnie . . ."

"Yes?"

"Ronnie, look at me."

She turned her head, and Sam's brown eyes searched hers. She smiled. "You're still worried about me, aren't you?"

He nodded. "You're in love with him, aren't you?"

Ronnie started to say, "Don't be ridiculous," but she swallowed against a sudden lump and whispered, "Yes."

His hand tightened on her shoulder. "Be careful, Ronnie. Don't let him hurt you."

"I won't."

"Just remember I'll be here if you need me."

"I know," she said. Then she lifted her head, and in a calm voice, she said, "I'll be back later. I want to get over to the hospital to see Laurie."

Ronnie pushed open the door to Room #315, and the smells of antiseptic and pine cleaner assailed her. There were two women in the room. One, a dark-haired, large-boned young woman, lay propped up in the bed nearest the door while she watched the television set mounted on the wall. She smiled at Ronnie, and Ronnie smiled back.

In the bed near the windows, Ronnie could see Laurie, who lay on her side facing the windows. Ronnie walked to her and around the bed.

"Hi, Laurie," she said.

Laurie's watery blue eyes stared up at her. Her hair had been brushed back from her forehead, and the purplish bruise looked even angrier. Her mouth was swollen and discolored. She closed her eyes.

"Can you talk?" asked Ronnie.

Laurie shrugged.

Ronnie could feel her hopelessness and despair. Anger flooded through her. Damn that Pete! How could he do this to a woman he professed to love? What was wrong with a man when he could allow himself to beat his wife and children? What perverse pleasure did this give him? "Do you mind if I sit here for a while?"

"No," Laurie whispered, then winced.

"Look, Laurie, I know you're in pain, so don't try to talk any more than you have to. I just wanted you to know what's happened. Pete ran away when he heard us coming, and so far we haven't tracked him down. But when we do, in order to get help for him, you've got to press charges."

"No." Laurie shook her head. "I won't."

"Laurie, please be sensible. If Pete doesn't get help, one of these times he might kill you or one of the kids."

"H . . . he'd never hurt the boys," Laurie said.

"He hurt one of them today!"

Laurie's eyes widened. "H . . . he never!"

"Oh, yes, he did," Ronnie said. She quickly explained what had happened and where she'd taken the boys. "And you can go to Sam's house, too, when you're better. You can stay with him until you can get on your feet, Laurie."

"H . . . how will I t . . . take care of myself?" Laurie whispered. "I never had a job." A tear slipped from one eye and slid down her pale cheek.

The sing-song voice of the hospital's paging system mixed in with the soft canned laughter of the television set.

"I'll help you. I promise."

She reached for Laurie's hand. The two women looked at each other for a long moment; then Ronnie squeezed Laurie's hand tightly in silent sympathy and understanding.

"I'm proud of you, Veronica," Alex said as Ronnie finished telling him about the happenings of the day.

"I didn't do anything," she said. "Just my job." But her eyes sparkled with pleasure at his approval.

"You did. You went that extra mile for that woman. You could have just sent her off to the hospital and let the county worry about her kids. Instead you tried to help her." Ronnie might look as if she needed someone to take care of her, but Alex now knew better. She was a strong woman, with strong emotions and a sense of commitment to her job and her town. She was a wonderful woman.

"I wish I knew where Pete Jacobsen went," she said with a sigh.

"He'll probably come skulking back to town. His kind never goes far. He'll whine and cry and expect his wife to take him back again."

"I hope she doesn't. Not unless he gets help."

"Did you persuade her to press charges?"

"She won't." Ronnie frowned, and her beautiful blue eyes clouded with worry. "She's agreed to leave him, but she doesn't want him to be 'put away,' as she calls it."

"What will she do? How will she support herself?"

"I've promised to help her," Ronnie said.

"Do you have any idea how?"

"No." Ronnie sighed. "I made the promise on the spur-of-the-moment, without really thinking." She bit her lip, and Alex suddenly wanted to make love to her. "But now that I think of it, maybe I could talk to Ed Traymore over at the hardware store. When I was in there the other day, I noticed how shorthanded he is now that his oldest daughter has to stay home and help her mother so much. Maybe he'd be willing to give Laurie a chance."

Alex stroked her neck, then pulled her toward him. "I can't wait another minute," he said. "I've been thinking about kissing you ever since you walked through the door tonight."

"Just kissing?" Ronnie teased.

"Well . . . maybe a bit more than kissing . . ." Her lips parted, and Alex was flooded with the desire to keep her there, in his arms, forever. If only we could close out the rest of the world, he thought. If only I could stop time. Then he quit thinking and let himself drown in the sweet taste and feel of her.

* * *

"But why do you have to go home?" Alex asked as he watched Ronnie pull on her red shorts and tie her halter top around her breasts.

"Because I told the department to call me the minute they find Pete, and I don't want them to call me in the middle of the night and not find me home," Ronnie said. She slipped her feet into her white moccasins.

"But you have a beeper," Alex protested. He sat up against the brass headboard, and his tanned chest glistened with sweat. The night was hot and muggy, and the opened window didn't help much.

"But if they have to call me by my beeper, they'll know I'm not home, won't they?" she asked reasonably.

"So what?"

"I don't want them to know."

"You said everyone is probably talking about us anyway," he insisted stubbornly. He patted the bed next to him. "Come back where you belong."

Ronnie had turned to leave, but his words stopped her. That's just it, she thought. I don't really belong there. I'm only a temporary occupant. She turned to face him. "Alex, you'll leave this town soon, but I have to live here. Yes, I think they're all talking about us and speculating, but that's not the same as *knowing*. I don't want them to know. I don't want them gossiping about me and feeling sorry for me when you're gone."

His eyes dropped, and he made no further protest.

"Good night, Alex. I'll see you tomorrow," she said softly; then she walked out of the room and out of the house.

But once she'd undressed and turned on her window air conditioner and climbed into her lonely bed, she couldn't fall asleep.

Now it was only seven more days before he'd be gone. And he *would* leave. She'd had a tiny glimmer of hope all along—hope that something would happen, something would change, and Alex would stay with her. But tonight that hope had been extinguished. She'd given him an opportunity to tell her she was wrong—that he wouldn't leave, that he loved her, that they'd work something out—and he hadn't. He hadn't denied her assertion that he'd go soon, and she would be the one to face the town and their talk.

Everyone will feel sorry for me. I won't be able to hide how I feel. I'll die inside when he goes, and everyone will know how miserable I am.

Why can't Alex love me? she wondered. I know he wants me, but that's not the same as loving me. Did he still love his wife? He'd said he didn't when he'd told her about Margo, but Ronnie wasn't sure if he even knew how he felt himself. Maybe Ronnie had simply been convenient for him, someone to ease the loneliness.

How could any man ever entirely forget a woman like Margo? She'd been gorgeous, with a face and body that could turn heads, a woman desired by every man who looked at her. She'd been all the things Ronnie wasn't.

On and on her thoughts swirled. Even if he did tell her he loved her, what difference would that make? A declaration of his feelings wouldn't change their circumstances. He was a famous playwright and he lived in New York City—where he belonged. She was a county sheriff, and she lived far away from the bright lights—where she belonged. He couldn't leave his life for her, and she couldn't leave Juliette. Aside from the fact that she'd hate living in the city, she had an obligation to the town and its people—people like Laurie Jacobsen, who was depending on her, and Sam, who loved her. Ronnie had worked hard to gain the respect of her constituents, to build her career. How could she just toss it all away?

And a long-distance romance would never work. And after awhile, they'd get sick of only seeing each other sporadically. Ronnie wanted to get married and have children. She wanted a normal life in Juliette with a man who loved her.

Was it possible that Alex might consider moving to Juliette? No. Even though he'd been happy there this summer, it was only because he needed the peace and isolation. But soon he'd be completely healed, and then he'd be happy to go back to his milieu. And when he was ready for a woman in his life, she'd be sophisticated and glamorous, and she'd love living in New York City and being the wife of a famous playwright.

Well, thought Ronnie, since I know all that, why did I try to make him feel bad tonight? Why not just let him go? Without guilt, without remorse, without any recriminations.

Finally she fell asleep, but her dreams were troubled, filled with images of Alex, and several times she whimpered softly.

* * *

Alex stood outside in the heavy night air. He couldn't sleep, but standing out here wasn't much of an improvement over tossing restlessly in his bed. The moon was almost completely obscured by scudding clouds. The air smelled of impending rain. Somewhere off in the distance he heard the wail of a siren. He looked up at Ronnie's apartment. The drone of her air conditioner cut through the silence. Her windows were dark.

He wished he were up there with her. If she hadn't made that remark about the people of the town talking about her once he was gone, he would have asked to go home with her.

Alex closed his eyes and leaned against the cool brick of the carriage house. He forced himself to think about leaving Juliette. Leaving Ronnie. God, he could hardly stand it being away from her for one night, let alone the rest of his life. But how could a permanent relationship between them work? Was he capable of committing himself to her wholeheartedly? Could he ever allow himself to do that again? Another failure would destroy him. Uncertainty mixed with fear filled his mind.

The crunch of gravel startled him. His eyes popped open.

"Sam? Is that you?" he called softly.

There was no answer, and Alex listened for a few minutes, but heard no other sound. It must have been my imagination, he thought. Or maybe that blasted cat, Hector, was prowling again. Sam had been falling down on his promise to keep the cat confined, and Alex had had another run-in with the belligerent feline a few days before.

Alex sighed heavily. He'd better go in, try to get some sleep. A raindrop slapped his forehead, and in the distance, thunder rumbled.

Alex pushed open the door and walked down the hall to the living room. Maybe he'd just pour himself a snifter of brandy. That'll help me sleep, he thought. The curtains in the living room windows billowed like ghosts in the sudden wind. The cooling air felt good against his skin, and Alex sank into a chair close to the window and took a sip of his brandy.

Suddenly he heard a deafening crash from the direction of the main house. It sounded like wood splintering and glass breaking. He jumped up, and the brandy glass flew out of his hand and shattered on the tile floor. Ignoring the broken glass, Alex raced to the front door and pushed it open. As he ran outside, lightning flashed against the charcoal sky, and in the sudden illumination he saw Ronnie's back door swaying drunkenly on its hinges.

"Oh, my God!" he said. Someone had broken into her apartment. His heart pounded. And as he raced to her stairs, taking them two at a time, the rain exploded from the sky.

NINE

Alex burst into Ronnie's apartment. Rain cascaded down in furious sheets, and lightning crackled and popped like gunfire. The noise of the sudden storm almost obscured the noise coming from the direction of Ronnie's bedroom, but Alex turned unerringly toward the sounds of the scuffle, then pitched headfirst toward the floor as his feet stumbled over an obstacle.

Alex winced against the sharp pain in his shin and scrambled to his feet. In the flashes of light from the storm he saw he'd tripped over a kitchen chair lying on its side in the middle of the floor.

"Ronnie!" he shouted, fear rising like bile in his throat.

"Alex!"

Her answering call propelled him. He raced to the bedroom, pushed open the door and lunged at the dark figure standing over someone lying in a heap on the floor. As he grabbed the intruder, Ronnie's breathless voice said, "Alex! Let me go!"

Only then did he realize the arms he had imprisoned were soft, feminine arms. Only then did he start to shake with delayed reaction.

"Oh, God, Ronnie. You're all right." He pulled her closer and ran his hands up and down her arms. "You're all right."

"Of course I'm all right. Let me go. Let me turn on a light," she said.

Seconds later soft lamplight revealed the limp body of a strange man lying on the beige carpet next to Ronnie's bed.

"What happened?" Alex said as he pulled Ronnie back to the safe circle of his arms. Her small body trembled as he pulled her close and stroked her hair. Dressed in a short satin nightgown the color of roses, she looked too small and too lovely to have overpowered the wiry intruder. Alex's heart still beat erratically, residue of the fear he'd felt.

"That's Pete Jacobsen. He must have kicked open my back door," Ronnie said. "I heard the noise; then I heard lightning and thunder and rain, and it seemed as if everything was happening at once."

"Did he hurt you?" I'll kill him if he did, Alex thought.

"No. He just scared me. He was shouting for Laurie. I guess he thought she was here, but he was so drunk, I'm not sure what he thought. I grabbed my gun from the dresser drawer when I heard the break-in, and when he came lurching into the bedroom I hit him over the head with the butt of the gun."

"That's it?" Alex said. "You hit him over the head, and he just fell down?"

Ronnie chuckled softly. "Sounds a little anticlimactic, doesn't it?"

"Oh, God, I don't care. All I care about is you. You're safe, and that's all that matters." He didn't know what he'd have done if she hadn't been safe. Even the thought caused him to tighten his arms around her. He closed his eyes and breathed in the smell of her.

"Alex . . ."

"What?" He kissed her hair.

"Please, Alex . . . let me go. I've got to call the department . . . tell them what happened."

Alex sat on the chair by her dressing table and watched as she picked up the phone by her bedside. While she calmly explained the night's events, he tried to make sense of his jumbled thoughts and emotions. She was magnificent. Just look at her. Calm, rational, sitting there like nothing happened. Her dark curls were in wild disarray, and her face was flushed and her clear blue eyes gleamed. He wanted to gather her in his arms again and make wild love to her. Kiss her and touch her and hold her and make her call out with pleasure. He wanted to keep her with him, protect her and love her.

That was it. Love her.

I love her.

Happiness exploded through his body like the rain exploding through the night sky, careening through his mind and heart.

I love her.

He watched as she stood up. Pete Jacobsen stirred. Ronnie looked at Alex.

"Don't worry," Alex said. "I'll sit on him if he moves a muscle."

"Good." She smiled, and Alex's heart caught at the sheer delight of watching her smile. "I'd better get dressed before the guys get here."

Alex smiled as she raised the nightgown and lifted it over her head, revealing her tiny, perfect body. It never stopped pleasing him to know Ronnie wasn't shy around him. She quickly donned panties and bra, then pulled on a pair of white cotton pants and a red T-shirt. She shoved her feet into the white moccasins she'd worn earlier and picked up her hairbrush, giving her hair a few careless swipes. She'd taken only about two minutes to dress, but in Alex's eyes, she looked as good as any model or actress who prepared for hours to face the cameras.

Forty-five minutes later, after the deputies had taken Pete Jacobsen away, and Sam, who had finally awakened at the sound of sirens, had gone back to bed, Ronnie sank down on the side of her bed and sighed.

"Thank goodness that's over," she said. She looked at her bedside clock. "Good grief. It's four o'clock. We'll both be exhausted tomorrow."

"I don't feel tired," Alex said. He felt too excited, too energized by the knowledge of his love for this fabulous woman. In fact, he probably wouldn't be able to sleep at all.

"I don't either," Ronnie said ruefully. "Too much adrenaline still pumping through me, I guess."

"Come home with me," Alex said. "I don't want

to leave you." He saw her start to protest, knew she wanted to say she could take care of herself. He raised his hand. "I know you don't need me to look after you. That's not what I meant."

"What *did* you mean?" Her eyes darkened as they captured his.

Alex could see the little pulse beating in her throat. The room felt charged with electricity as the rain pelted her windows. "I meant I couldn't bear the thought of leaving you, of being without you," he whispered.

He saw her eyes close for a second. When she raised her lashes and looked at him again, her eyes sparkled with the sheen of tears. She swallowed, and Alex had difficulty breathing. She wet her lips, and her face twisted. She stood and turned her back to him.

"Don't turn away from me, Ronnie." He covered the distance between them in two strides, grabbed her shoulders and spun her around. "Don't ever turn away from me again."

Her lower lip trembled; and Alex, filled with a longing to comfort and love her, lowered his mouth, capturing her soft lips with his. An overwhelming love surged through him as he felt the desperation and need in her response.

They tumbled onto her narrow bed, and the fury of their lovemaking seemed one with the fury of the storm raging outside. Finally, when the violence outside spent itself, the violence inside subsided, and the lovers fell asleep wrapped in each other's arms.

* * *

"Don't go to work today," Alex coaxed. "They'll understand. Stay with me. We have so much to talk about."

The pleading light in his soft, gray eyes was difficult to resist, but Ronnie shook her head. "I have to. It's my responsibility. What happened last night is just part of my job."

Alex sighed, and Ronnie smiled. Sometimes he reminded her of a little boy when he didn't get his way. "Well . . . okay," he said. His crooked half-smile tugged at her heart. "But come over right after work. I have a lot to tell you. And something important to ask you."

Ronnie's heart leaped into her throat. He looked so serious. Could he mean . . . ? All her hazy dreams seemed to float in her mind. She nodded her head. "All right." Her voice sounded strange to her ears. She cleared her throat. "Now, get out of here, and let me get ready."

As Alex turned to leave he said, "I'll be thinking about you all day."

Ronnie hugged herself as he left. Me, too, she thought. Me, too.

Alex hadn't thought he'd be able to accomplish any work that day, but surprisingly he had. He'd settled down to the final revisions of Act III about eleven that morning, and now, at three, it looked as if he were finished. He leaned back in his chair and stretched. The muscles of his neck ached from leaning over the typewriter for hours.

He stood up and did some stretching exercises to

relieve the tension. God, that felt good. Now he'd take a shower and put on fresh clothes; then he'd rummage through the freezer and see what he could fix for dinner. Or should he take Ronnie out? When you were planning to tell a woman you loved her and wanted to marry her, wasn't it appropriate to take her out to a romantic restaurant?

No. He'd pick flowers and light candles here. He wanted them to be alone so they could make love after they talked . . . make love without waiting to drive home and all that nonsense. He smiled. Veronica Valetti. A beautiful name for a beautiful woman. The woman he loved.

Humming to himself, Alex walked back to the bedroom. Just as he put his foot into the tub, the phone shrilled. Swearing softly, he padded out to the living room, picked up the phone and said, "Yes?"

"Alex?"

It was Bernie. Alex grinned. Wouldn't old Bernie be surprised when he found out? "Hello, Bernie."

"So how's the rewrite comin'? Just about done?"

"I *am* done."

"No kiddin'! That's great, kid."

Alex frowned. Bernie didn't sound as happy or excited as Alex had imagined he would. "Something wrong, Bernie?" he asked.

"Depends on how you look at it," Bernie said.

"How I look at what?"

"You sittin' down?" Bernie barked.

"No. As a matter of fact, I was just about to get into the shower. I'm standing in the middle of the living room, bare bones naked, with all the windows wide open."

"Tryin' to give the town a thrill, eh, kid?"

"Come on, Bernie. Don't hedge. Something's wrong. What is it?"

He heard Bernie sigh. "Hell, I might as well just give it to you straight. Margo's back."

Alex's breath caught painfully. A vision of her glittering golden-brown eyes and perfect cameo face flashed in his mind. A knot twisted in his gut. Then a second image superseded the first. This time he saw dark curly hair framing a small face and brilliant blue eyes filled with love. He took a deep breath. Margo's memory no longer had the power to hurt him. Ronnie loved him. He was sure of it. And he loved her. He was finally finished with the past.

"Say somethin'," Bernie said gruffly.

Alex knew Bernie was worried. "I'm okay, Bernie. I don't give a damn whether she's back or not."

"Well . . ."

"Well, what?"

"Well . . . that's not all."

"What do you mean?"

"I mean she's not alone."

Why was Bernie talking in riddles? "So? I'm sure she hasn't been alone since the moment she left me." Knowing Margo, she'd been surrounded by men eager to take his place.

"She has a little boy with her, and she says he's your son."

Alex stopped breathing. His blood pounded in his ears. His son! He squeezed his eyes shut.

"Alex?"

The voice seemed to come from far away. Alex opened his mouth to speak, but nothing came out.

"Alex!"

This time Bernie shouted, and Alex took a ragged breath. "I . . . I don't understand," he said.

"It's simple. She had a kid after she left you, and she says it's yours."

"I . . . I don't believe it." Could it be true? Alex had always wanted children of his own. It was a wish never articulated but deeply felt. "Have you seen the boy? How old is he?"

"Nah. I haven't seen him yet, but she seemed like she was tellin' the truth. I believed her."

Alex knew Bernie disliked Margo, so if he felt she were telling the truth, she must have been very convincing. "What do you think I should do?" he said.

"I think you should pack up and come home right now. Take care of this. See what she wants."

"I . . . I'll have to think about it, Bernie. It's not the best time for me to leave."

"Why not? You said you were finished with the rewrite."

"I know, but something else has come up." How could he leave Ronnie now? Nothing was settled between them. But how could he ask her to marry him until he saw Margo and this child she claimed was his? "Listen, Bernie," he said. "I'll call you back later. Let me think about it for a while."

"Okay, kid, but I think you better decide to come. This won't wait."

Ronnie wanted to look as pretty as she possibly could. Something told her this night would be the most important night of her life. Happiness and anticipation danced within her, and the excitement had flooded her face with color and her eyes with stars. She fingered her white cotton sundress edged with white lace. It was a dress she saved for special occasions. After carefully applying makeup and dabbing Joy everywhere, she looked at herself in the mirror. Her eyes were shining, and she looked almost beautiful. She blew herself a kiss for luck. Then she raced down the back steps.

When Alex opened the door, she smiled. He looked so handsome and so solemn. He took her hand and led her into the living room. Ronnie stood transfixed as her eyes took in the welter of packed suitcases and boxes, but her brain refused to process the information.

She stared at him. Her heart thudded painfully against her chest. Her knees felt weak. She clutched the arm of the nearest chair. I won't cry, she told herself. I won't.

"Ronnie, darling, sit down. Don't look like that," Alex said.

The "darling" barely registered. But his next words did. Stunning in their impact, they demolished her dreams and sent them crashing down in ruins at her feet.

As Alex slowly explained about Bernie's phone call, Ronnie began to feel numb inside. "A . . . a son," she stammered. A son. *Her* child. Their child. The words pummeled Ronnie's brain like hailstones on a tin roof. She felt lightheaded, and she turned and sank down on the chair.

Alex sat on the arm of the chair and touched her shoulder. He kissed the top of her head.

"Oh, Ronnie, I'm sorry," he said. "I'd give anything if this hadn't happened, but it doesn't make any difference, really. All it means is I have to go back to the city early and take care of this . . . get things straightened out."

"I understand," she said. Her heart felt frozen in her chest. She couldn't look up at him. She twisted her hands in her lap. *I must stay calm. I mustn't let him see how upset I am.*

"Ronnie, please look at me," he begged.

She heard the pleading in his voice, but she couldn't allow herself to accept any comfort from him. If he were to put his arms around her or kiss her, she knew she'd break down. And once she started crying, she might never stop. "It's quite all right, Alex. Of course, you must go. I wouldn't think much of you if you didn't."

"This doesn't change anything between us, Ronnie," he said. "Please believe that. I'll just go down there and get this mess straightened out—see where I stand and what Margo wants—then I'll be back. We still have things to discuss—to settle."

Ronnie jumped up. She forced herself to look him straight in the eye. She saw the uncertainty. She had to make it easy for him. This was inevitable. For just awhile there, she'd allowed herself to dream, but dreams were just that. Dreams weren't reality. This was reality. Alex . . . going back to his world . . . his son . . . the woman he'd never forgotten. Ronnie knew once Alex saw Margo again, saw her with their son, all would be lost. This had been a magical interlude, something to remember the rest of her life . . . but it wasn't real life. Real life was Juliette, her job, her friends, her family, ordinary things in an ordinary world. Eventually, she'd forget Alex. She'd have to forget him. She had no choice.

"I always knew you'd go back to your world," she said. "I just wasn't prepared for it tonight. It . . . it was a shock at first, but I'm fine now." She smiled to show how fine she was.

"Ronnie . . ." He reached, touched her shoulders.

She shrank back. "Please, Alex. Please, don't. I really think it would be best if I go home, and you can finish up and get out of here."

"I wasn't planning to leave until morning," he said. "Can't we have tonight together?"

Ronnie shook her head. "I don't think so." She had to get out of there. "It was different before. I . . . I just can't . . ." She extended her hand. "Goodbye, Alex. I'll never forget you."

"Goddamnit, Ronnie. Quit talking to me in that frozen voice, like I'm a stranger or something! Try to understand. I have to go back right now, but I don't love Margo, and I'm not going back to her. I . . . I . . ." He stopped and ran his hands through his hair.

Ronnie's heart galloped. For a moment she thought he was going to say, "I love you."

"Ronnie, trust me," he said. "I've never lied to you, have I?"

"No." Not knowingly, she thought.

"Well, I'm not lying to you now. You *must* believe me. I *will* be back. As soon as I get this problem sorted out and put behind me."

"You'll never put this completely behind you,

Alex. You have a son." A son that will bind him to Margo forever, she thought.

"I'm not even sure the child is mine," he said. "That's another reason I have to go now and get it over with." His warm hands enveloped hers. "A few months ago, I might have been afraid to face Margo again—afraid of my feelings, afraid to confront the old hurts. But knowing you has changed me in so many ways. You're so brave, you have so much courage. You look life straight in the eye. You're not afraid of anything. You've helped me regain my strength by your example."

You're wrong, Alex, she cried inside. I'm desperately afraid of life without you. But she lifted her chin, smiled, and said, "I'm proud to be the one to have helped you realize your own strength, Alex. But you've always had it. You'd have found it on your own. It just might have taken longer." She tugged her hands from his. "Now I really must go home. And you must leave."

She stood up, and he rose with her. His hands clasped her shoulders. "I wanted this night to be so special," he said. Then he bent to kiss her, and Ronnie didn't have the strength to pull away.

Just one more time, she thought. She lost herself in the bittersweet magic of the kiss, knowing the memory of it would have to last her a lifetime.

After Ronnie left, Alex felt like throwing things. Why, why did this have to happen now? He knew he'd never be able to sleep, so he decided to load his car and leave that night. He wrote a check and a short note to Sam, put them both in an envelope and sealed it, then went out front to pull the car up to the door.

After loading his bags and boxes in the trunk and back seat, he walked up to the front of the house and knocked on Sam's screen door. As he waited for Sam to answer, he looked around.

The lowering sun slanted through the green porch awnings, and on the far railing sat Hector like a king on his throne, his golden-green eyes glowing in a riveting stare.

As Alex's eyes met his, Hector hissed, and his coppery fur stood at attention.

Alex smiled wryly. Like master, like cat, he thought. Neither one liked him much.

"Hello, Alex." Sam's pudgy body was visible through the screen. There was no warmth in his voice.

"Hello, Sam," Alex said. "I brought you this." He held out the envelope.

Sam pushed the screen door open, and the hinges squeaked. "You leavin'?"

"Yes, I've been called away rather suddenly. I wrote the check out to cover the utilities and telephone. You have the deposit to cover any damage you might find. I also put my address and telephone number in New York inside so that you can call me if you need to."

Alex turned to leave, then stopped. He turned around slowly. Sam stood there, unmoving and unblinking, disdain written on his face. Alex hesitated, then said, "You'll look after Ronnie while I'm gone?"

"I've been lookin' after Ronnie for a long time . . . long before you came on the scene, and I'll be lookin' after her long after you're gone," he said coldly.

Alex wished he could tell Sam he was wrong. I love her even more than you do, he wanted to say. But he didn't. Instead he said, "Thank you. I've enjoyed living in the carriage house. It's been an unforgettable summer."

Sam didn't answer. Alex could feel his eyes staring at him as he walked away.

Later, as the powerful car devoured the miles between Juliette and New York City effortlessly, Alex replayed the scene with Ronnie over and over in his mind. He hoped she believed him. He hoped he was right not to have said anything about their future together. He had to be free of all encumbrances before he could make a life with Ronnie. He knew he was right. After he saw Margo, he could call Ronnie, and he could go back to Juliette. Then everything would be the way it should be.

All I have to do, he told himself, is get through the next few days. See the boy, try to determine if Margo's telling the truth about him. See her. Exorcize the demons. His plan sounded simple. So why was his stomach knotted with fear?

TEN

Two days later, the same knot of fear twisted his insides as Alex rang the doorbell of Apartment #32E in the luxurious Park Avenue building. He heard the melodius chimes echo on the other side of the door.

Smoothing a nonexistent wrinkle from his immaculate beige slacks, he wet his lips and took a deep breath. There's no reason to feel afraid or nervous, he told himself for the dozenth time.

The door whispered open. A young Spanish maid dressed in a blue uniform and white apron smiled shyly.

"Alex Summerfield to see Miss McKenna," Alex said. He attempted to smile but knew the effort fell far short.

"Si, senor. Please to come in. Meez Mahkenna, she expects you." The maid turned and walked briskly across the parquet foyer, through a set of double walnut doors and into an enormous living room. Alex could see the windows afforded a spectacular view of New York's skyline.

"Alex!"

He would have known that lilting, musical voice anywhere. Margo stood up and waited for him to approach her. Against the black and white color scheme of the modern apartment, her vivid coloring looked even more striking than usual. The golden-brown eyes, which once had the power to mesmerize him, sparkled with the brilliance of topaz. The fiery hair, a shade of copper found in newly minted pennies, shot dazzling prisms of color in the sun's rays. The oval face with its translucent skin and creamy perfection glowed with health and loving care. The magnificent body he'd known so well didn't look as if she could ever have borne a child. Dressed today in pale yellow linen, she looked as if she'd just stepped out of the pages of *Vogue*.

"Hello, Margo," he said.

She smiled—the same fetchingly beautiful smile that had always had the power to melt his resolve, to win anything she'd ever wanted from him . . . or anyone else. Then she held out her arms, thin gold bracelets jingling, and Alex hesitated an almost imperceptible moment.

Like a sleepwalker, he opened his arms, and she moved into them, lifting her face for his kiss. The same scent of jasmine she'd always favored filled his senses. The knot tightened as he met her lips.

At the first touch of her cool lips, relief flooded Alex's body. The knot loosened, and with a heady feeling of freedom, Alex gave her a sound, friendly kiss—the kind he might give any dear friend he hadn't seen in years. Confidence returned as he gently held her at arm's length.

"You look . . . gorgeous . . . as usual," he said with a smile. "I'd almost forgotten how beautiful you are." He could say it without torment, as if he were admiring an exquisite painting, nothing more. She no longer had the power to devastate him. Only a small, dark-haired, blue-eyed vixen could make him feel helplessly enslaved now. The thought of Ronnie warmed Alex, and his smile widened.

"And you, my handsome ex-husband, still have that knock-'em-dead, make-their-knees-turn-to-jelly appeal," she said with a merry chuckle.

"How have you been?" he asked.

"I'm terrific . . . really terrific," she said. "Why don't we sit down?" She gestured to the long white couch. "Would you like a drink?"

Alex shook his head. He wanted to see the boy.

As if reading his mind, her eyes glittered knowingly, and she said, "You're anxious to meet your son, aren't you?"

Alex wasn't ready to concede his acceptance of parentage, so he chose his words carefully. "I'd like to see the boy, yes. It . . . it's hard for me to believe I have a son. I don't understand why you never wrote to tell me about him."

She ran the tip of her pink tongue over her bottom lip and gave him a thoughtful look. "It's a long story. We'll talk about all that later. Let me go and get Christopher."

Christopher. Christopher had been Margo's father's name.

It seemed like hours before she returned with a chubby toddler in her arms. Alex stiffened as she moved from the shadows into the sunlight; then his heart seemed to stop. For a long moment he couldn't speak.

There could be no denial of this child. He felt as if he were looking at his own baby pictures. The same inky black hair and the identical cleft chin hammered the message home. *This is your son. Your son.* The only difference in the face Alex stared at now and the face he stared at in the mirror each morning was the color of their eyes. Christopher's eyes were the same golden-flecked brown as his mother's, and right now they stared at Alex with bright curiosity, although he kept his sturdy arms wrapped tightly around Margo's neck.

"May I?" Alex asked, a husky catch in his voice. He held out his arms.

"Certainly. Christopher, darling, this is your father." Margo loosened the child's arms and held him out to Alex.

Christopher's eyes widened with momentary alarm, and he whimpered.

"It's okay, son," Alex said softly. He enfolded the child in his arms. The feel of the warm, strong body, and the smell of boy, an odor Alex had forgotten, permeated his senses. Pride and love expanded his chest. "I'm your father."

"Fodder," Christopher said. Then, as Alex's heart twisted, Christopher twined his chubby arms around Alex's neck and burrowed his head under Alex's chin. Alex blinked against the sudden tears that misted his eyes. His arms tightened.

"H . . . how old is he?" Alex asked.

"Eighteen months," she said and smiled. She had the look of satisfaction Alex associated with a well-fed cat. "He's the spitting image of you, Alex."

She knew I was doubting her story. Alex lowered himself to the couch but still held Christopher tightly.

"So, what do you think?" she asked as she crossed one perfectly shaped leg over the other.

There were undercurrents Alex didn't understand. What did she want? "About what?" he hedged.

"About being a father, silly!" Her tinkling laugh hovered between them.

"I'm overwhelmed." Christopher had snuggled up against Alex's chest. He smoothed the child's thick hair and answered her question as truthfully as he could. "I wish I'd known about his existence sooner. I think I had the right to know."

"Oh, Alex, don't look at me that way." She pouted prettily, a mannerism calculated to melt any man's heart, as Alex well knew.

"I'm not going to belabor the point, Margo. What's done is done. But I guess the question is: what do you want?"

"Want?" The shining eyes widened. "Why . . . I *want* my son to know his father, that's what I *want*."

"Are you planning to move back to New York, then?"

She lifted her shoulders in a dainty shrug. "I'm not sure. . . ."

"How long did you plan to stay?"

She studied him thoughtfully. "I guess that depends on you."

"Is it money?" he said bluntly.

She shook her head. "No. It's not money. Although I did think you'd want to support Christopher."

"Of course I want to support Christopher! That's not what I meant, and you know it."

"Don't get upset, Alex," she soothed.

"I'm not upset, damnit!"

"Don't swear in front of Christopher," she said.

Alex gritted his teeth. Christopher wriggled, and Alex released him, setting him gently on the floor.

"Go see Patty," Christopher said. He grinned, and Alex's heart squeezed.

There was no way Alex would allow her to take Christopher back to Europe. No way. At that moment, he knew he wanted this child. To keep Christopher close, Alex would be willing to sacrifice anything. Ronnie's smiling face popped into his mind. Almost anything, he qualified.

"All right, darling," Margo said. "You go see Patty."

Both parents watched as the toddler trudged off. Once the dark head was out of sight, they turned back to each other.

"Who's Patty?" Alex asked distractedly, more for something to say than because he really wanted to know.

"Rosamond's puppy." Rosamond Gregg was an old friend of Margo's, and this sumptuous apartment belonged to her. "She makes him stay in the kitchen because he's not completely housetrained."

"Where is Rosamond?"

"She had a luncheon date. She'll be back later." Margo smiled a little half-smile. "She told me she thought we might like to have the place to ourselves for the big reunion."

"Do you want to get back together? Is that what this is all about?"

The question reverberated in the air between them. Alex held his breath.

"Not exactly. . . ."

"What *do* you want?" Alex insisted. His stomach muscles tensed.

Margo sighed. "Let's just say I want you and your son to get to know one another. For now I plan to stay for a month or so, and then . . . after you've had a chance to spend time with Christopher . . . we'll talk again. How does that suit you?"

It didn't suit him at all, but what choice did he have? He didn't know anything about family law, and he wasn't sure of his legal rights. He couldn't afford to make her angry. Good sense dictated caution, because now that his son had been given to him, Alex didn't think he could bear giving him up. He'd call Bernie as soon as he got back to his apartment. Bernie knew the best lawyers in town. This would be the last time he'd be at a disadvantage when talking to Margo. The next time they met, he'd have the upper hand.

Alex stared at Russell Cookson, the family law expert Bernie had recommended. "Do you mind repeating what you just said?"

"Certainly not," the lawyer said. He pushed his thick glasses back up his nose and cleared his throat. "I said, Mr. Summerfield, that it really doesn't mat-

OPENING ACT / 181

ter what you think or what you want. Unless your name appears on the child's birth certificate as the father, you haven't got any rights at all."

Alex's heart pounded. He clenched his teeth and glared at the lawyer as if he were the one preventing Alex from attaining his goal.

"Unless, of course . . ." the lawyer continued slowly, biting on the end of his pencil as he talked, "you were married to the mother when she gave birth. That would make all the difference. Then, you see, it wouldn't matter in the least who the father was—by law *you* would be the father. . . ."

"Goddamnit," Alex shouted, jumping to his feet. "Haven't you heard a word I said? I *am* the father!"

"It isn't necessary to shout at me, Mr. Summerfield," Cookson said reproachfully. "I am not hard of hearing."

"Sorry," Alex muttered as he sank back into the brown leather chair. He ran his hands through his hair. "It's just that I feel so helpless, and you didn't act as if you understood."

"I understand perfectly. What *you* fail to understand is that laws govern these kinds of situations, and in your particular situation, the law is clear-cut. If you and your ex-wife were already divorced when this child was born, unless the birth certificate specifies you as the father, you have no legal rights."

"And I can't do anything?" Alex asked wearily.

"There are any number of things you can try." Cookson lifted the pewter pitcher sitting on the left side of his desk and poured himself a glass of water. "Would you like some?" he asked politely.

"No, thanks." Why didn't the pompous old goat get to the point?

Cookson sipped his water. "Where was I? Oh, yes . . . well, the first and most obvious thing to do is simply ask your ex-wife to let you see a copy of the birth certificate."

"What if she refuses?"

"If you pretend you don't believe her story and that you want proof of the child's parentage, perhaps she'll see the wisdom of granting your request." Cookson leaned back in his chair with a pleased expression on his face.

It's all right for him to smile, Alex thought. It's not his kid we're talking about. To him this is just a legal problem, nothing more. "What else can I try?" Alex asked.

"Well, if she can't or won't produce the birth certificate, we can go to court and try to get the judge to order a blood test on the child. But that won't really solve your problem, because all a blood test can show beyond a doubt is if it's impossible for you to have fathered the boy. It can't tell us whether you did."

"I don't need any blood test to tell me he's my son. All anyone has to do is look at Christopher, and they'd know I'm the father," Alex insisted.

"That may be, Mr. Summerfield. But a strong resemblance is not proof, and it won't carry any weight in court, I'm afraid." He raised his hands, palms up, as if illustrating the shakiness of Alex's claim to Christopher. Then he frowned. "There *is* something else, though. . . ."

"Yes?" Alex leaned forward eagerly.

"Has your ex-wife mentioned money to you?"

"She suggested I might contribute to Christopher's support."

"Have you done so yet?"

Alex adopted his "be-serious" look. "I just talked to her yesterday afternoon, Mr. Cookson," he said dryly.

"Well, if she accepts money from you, she'll be acknowledging parentage. Yes . . . that's the best course to follow, I believe. Get her to accept money . . . write checks, of course, so you'll have proof later . . . and make sure the money is consistent . . . given to her on a regular basis over a period of months . . . then you'll have grounds with which to fight her if she later tries to remove the boy from your influence. . . ."

Months. Months. He didn't want to wait months. Then Alex sighed wearily. Well, at least it was something. And right now he was willing to try anything. But first he'd ask to see the birth certificate.

When the phone rang, Ronnie leaped up from the couch. Maybe it was Alex.

"Hello?" she said hopefully.

"Veronica?"

It *was* Alex. "Oh, Alex . . . hi."

"Hi." His voice had softened, and Ronnie's stomach felt like warm honey. "How are you?" he said.

"Oh, I'm fine," she said. *But I miss you. I miss you so much.*

"God, Ronnie, I miss you," he said.

Ronnie's heart tap danced. "Me, too," she whispered. "H . . . have you seen your son yet?"

"Yes. Yesterday."

He didn't sound happy. "Wh . . . what's wrong?" she asked.

"That obvious, huh?"

She smiled. She knew him so well now. Even the slightest nuance in his voice told her volumes. "Yes," she answered. She picked up the telephone and stretched the extension as far as it would go so she could sit back on the couch in comfort.

"Ronnie," he said. "Everything is a mess."

"In what way?"

He sighed, the sound carrying clearly across the wires. "Well, yesterday I went over to the apartment where Margo is staying, and I saw Christopher. There's no doubt he's my son, Ronnie. He looks exactly like me."

Ronnie swallowed. If there was no problem with the boy, there must be a problem with Margo. Oh, please, she prayed. Don't tell me you're going back with her.

". . . And I don't know what the hell she wants!"

"I . . . I'm sorry, Alex. What did you say?"

"I said, Margo is acting coy. I don't know what she wants from me, and I'm frustrated as hell. I even went to see a family law expert today to see what I could do about this impasse, and guess what?"

"What?"

"I can't do one blasted thing except ask to see Christopher's birth certificate. Aside from that, the only recourse I have is to get Margo to accept money from me on a regular basis. I might as well be any jerk on the street for all the rights I have." Then, in a calmer voice, he explained everything the lawyer had told him.

"Alex, I'm sorry. I know how frustrated you must feel."

"Frustrated isn't the word. I'm fit to be tied, if you'll pardon a trite expression. I'd like to strangle somebody—preferably Margo." He laughed, but the sound had a hopeless ring. "Oh, Ronnie, I wish you could see him." His voice lowered, became husky. "He's wonderful. I took one look at him and knew I couldn't let her take him away from me."

The lump in Ronnie's throat expanded, and she blinked back tears. An image of a little boy with Alex's impish grin and sparkling eyes shimmered in her mind. "Of course not," she whispered.

"I don't know what to do," he said sadly. "I thought it would only take a few days to straighten this out, and I intended to be on my way back to Juliette by the end of the week, but it looks as if it's going to take longer."

"I understand," she said. And she did understand. She understood perhaps better than he thought, perhaps better than he understood. He was still fighting the inevitable. He still thought the two of them could work out something, but Ronnie knew better. "Maybe she wants to get back together, Alex, and she's waiting until you're so completely captivated by Christopher that you'll agree to her terms."

His silence told her that he'd already thought of that possibility.

"So, when do rehearsals start?" she asked.

"The end of the month," he said distractedly. "Listen, Ronnie, you'll wait, won't you? We have to talk, but I can't come up there until I know where I am. I'm just not free to do anything right now."

"You know where to find me, Alex. I'm not going anywhere," Ronnie said quietly. She knew her answer wasn't exactly what he'd wanted to hear, but it was the best she could do right then.

Listlessly, Ronnie discarded the ten of spades, and Sam gleefully pounced on the card.

"Gin," he said as he laid down his hand.

Ronnie sighed. She put her own cards on the kitchen table and rubbed her forehead.

"Headache?"

"Yes," she murmured.

"I guess you don't want to play another?"

She shook her head. "I'm tired, Sam. Do you mind?"

When he didn't answer, she looked up to find his dark eyes fixed on her and concern etched into the lines of his face. "Have you heard from him lately?" he asked.

Ronnie knew he meant Alex. "Yes. He called last night."

"And?"

"Same as before. He doesn't know what his ex-wife wants. He's waiting for her to make a move. He's angry and frustrated. When he asked her to show him Christopher's birth certificate, she said she'd left it in her deposit box in Europe. Then he tried to set up regular child support payments. His lawyer told him if he could get Margo to accept money on a regular basis, it would establish his claim to parentage, but even there, Margo's been crafty. She always evades the issue and tells Alex they'll talk about it later. Alex is afraid to push her. He can't prove he's Christopher's father, and he's scared if he tries to get tough with her, she'll just pack up and leave, taking his son with her."

"And if she decides she wants to get back together, then what?"

That was the $64,000 question, Ronnie thought. The question that had haunted her the past eight weeks. Eight weeks. She stared pensively out the window. The trees blazed in their autumn finery—dressed in brilliant gold and scarlet and every variation in between. The entire world wore its party face, as if defying winter's approach.

Ronnie's heart felt like winter already. She moved blindly through the glorious days. Even the crisp, cool air didn't invigorate her as it had in the past. She felt numb, dead, full of grief and loss. Each day her residue of hope waned. Soon nothing would be left except resignation and pain.

She'd tried to hide her unhappiness, but she knew everyone talked about her behind her back. Some people—Miss Agatha, for instance—had confronted her head on.

Ronnie cringed, remembering that day shortly after Alex had left. Miss Agatha had come marching into Ronnie's office.

"Veronica," she'd said briskly as she pushed open

Ronnie's door. "May I see you for a few moments?" She placed her cane on the edge of Ronnie's desk and sat stiffly upright in the chair in front of the desk. Her dark eyes flashed as she settled her purple flowered dress around her legs.

Ronnie sat quietly, rolling her pen between her fingers as she waited.

"Well?" she snapped.

"Well, what?" Ronnie countered.

"Well, where is that scoundrel? Where has he gone?"

"You mean Alex?"

"Of course I mean Alex," said Miss Agatha, exasperation edging her voice.

"He's gone . . . gone home," Ronnie said quietly. The pain that always hovered at the edge of her consciousness pushed its way into her mind, and she wished everyone would leave her alone.

"Gone home!" Incredulity replaced exasperation, and Miss Agatha's mouth dropped open.

If Ronnie hadn't felt so miserable, she'd have laughed at the rare specter of Miss Agatha stunned into silence.

Finally Miss Agatha said, "And just when do you expect him to return?"

"I don't."

"What? Why ever not?"

"Because he was only visiting here for the summer. You know that. He always planned to go back to the city."

"Well!" Miss Agatha exploded. "After all I did to get the two of you together!"

OPENING ACT / 189

Suddenly, Miss Agatha's machinations made sense. Everything clicked into place in Ronnie's brain. Tears filled her eyes. She swallowed and bent her head. She heard Miss Agatha get up, and then the old lady was standing next to her. The poignantly delicate scent of lavender surrounded Ronnie as Miss Agatha patted Ronnie's head and murmured, "Now, now. It will be all right."

Ronnie wanted to throw herself into Miss Agatha's arms and cry and cry until there were no tears left. But she didn't. She clenched her teeth and willed herself to look up calmly. "I'm okay," she said.

"Whatever possessed that young man to leave? I just don't understand it," Miss Agatha said. Frowning, she walked back to her chair and reseated herself. "I thought the two of you were getting along so well."

"We were. It wasn't that. His ex-wife returned from Europe, and Alex found out he has a son by her. He went back to New York to see her and the boy."

"Well, fine. But surely he'll want you to join him there!"

"Miss Agatha, I know you mean well. I appreciate your concern, and I know your actions were motivated out of love for me, but I doubt anything permanent could ever work out for me and Alex. I think his ex-wife wants to reconcile, and from talking to Alex, I think he'd agree to those terms if that was the only way he could keep his son with him."

"What do you mean? Keep his son with him?"

"Well, she hasn't come right out and said it, but

his ex-wife has implied that she'll take little Christopher back to Europe if Alex doesn't go along with her."

"And she wants to resume their marriage?" The dark eyes narrowed.

Ronnie shrugged. "I don't know. But it wouldn't surprise me, and I think it would be best for us all if I just forget about Alex Summerfield." Her telephone buzzed, and Ronnie grimaced. "Look, Miss Agatha, you're going to have to excuse me. I've got a call."

The old lady stood, picked up her cane, and frowned. She walked out muttering, "I thought he had more sense!"

Oh, God, Ronnie thought. I've got to forget him.

But the conversation with Miss Agatha had taken place weeks ago, and now it was almost the end of October, and Ronnie was still hanging onto a shred of hope.

"Ronnie?" Sam reached across the kitchen table and grasped her hands. His touch was comforting. "You looked like you were a million miles away just now."

Not a million, she thought. Only a few hundred. "I'm sorry, Sam." Then she made a determined effort to look more cheerful, and in an effort to change the subject, she said brightly, "I saw Laurie today."

"You did! How's she doin'?"

"She looks great, and Ed Traymore told me she's doing a wonderful job for him."

"You know, Ronnie, you did a good piece of work when you persuaded her to press charges against Pete. Look how good everything's worked out."

Yes, Ronnie thought. Pete was doing well, too. The counselor in the alcohol abuse program at the county hospital had told Ronnie he'd responded well to the counseling sessions, and Laurie had told her that when she'd visited him a few days ago, he'd been like a different person.

"And I've got you to thank for all this, Ronnie," Laurie had said. Her blue eyes shone happily.

Laurie even looked prettier, Ronnie thought, now that she felt like a worthwhile person.

"Yes," Ronnie said in answer to Sam's comment. "I do feel good about what's happened with Laurie and Pete." At least someone's life seems to be working out, she thought wearily.

Sam smiled across the table at her. "You look awful tired tonight. Why don't I go home now? Then you take a couple of aspirins and go to bed. Okay?"

But after he left, Ronnie sat at the table and continued to stare out the window for a long time. The conversation with Sam had crystalized her situation in her mind. This limbo couldn't continue. Alex had asked her to wait awhile, and she had, although she'd known nothing would come of the waiting. Now two months had passed, and nothing new had developed, and until she could put this unhappiness behind her, Ronnie knew she'd continue to feel miserable.

I'm not the kind of person who can sit and wait, she thought. Maybe some women could but not me. Besides, Alex hadn't made any commitment to her. He hadn't made any promises. He'd never even said he loved her. Doubt settled like a storm cloud around Ronnie's heart. She was a fool to mope around, hoping and waiting. She had to take action. Otherwise I'll be no good to anyone, least of all myself, she thought.

Lifting her chin, she stood up, walked into the living room, picked up the phone, and dialed.

"Alex?" she said. She took a deep breath. "Alex, there's something I want to say, and I don't want you to interrupt me until I've said it."

"Ronnie, what's wrong?"

She heard the alarm, and yes, the fear, but she bit her lip and plunged ahead. "I'm through waiting, Alex. I can't live this way any longer. I have to get on with my life. And I think if you're honest you'll agree it'll be best for everyone if we say goodbye and part as friends. I want to remember what we had together this past summer. I don't want to remember our relationship as one of unhappiness and pain."

"Ronnie, please—"

"I've made a decision. I want you to stop calling me. I . . . I don't want to see you again."

ELEVEN

Alex slammed the receiver down, tension and frustration knotting the muscles in his neck and shoulders. Maisie had given him the runaround again. Ronnie wasn't in, she'd said. How could he talk to Ronnie if she refused to return his phone calls? And she'd gotten an answering machine, so that when he called her at home, all he ever heard was her voice on the taped message.

Listlessly, he walked over to the window of his apartment. The windows faced Central Park, and as he looked down he could see people everywhere. It was one of those cold, clear, crisp November days that usually made him so glad to be alive.

The last month had been hellish. He felt torn apart. Part of him longed to throw some clothes in a suitcase, throw the suitcase in his car, and take off for Juliette and Ronnie. The other part of him knew he had to stay right here in the city. He was desperately afraid if he left, even for a few days, Margo and Christopher would be gone when he got back.

He clenched his right fist and punched it into his left palm. The force of the blow hurt, but he ignored the pain. It felt good to hit something. Damn Margo! Why was she toying with him? Did she enjoy making him suffer? And surely she knew he *was* suffering.

In less than four weeks, it would be Christmas. I'm not going to wait a minute longer, he thought. I'm going to go over there and tell Margo in no uncertain terms just how it's going to be. I'm going to insist upon joint custody. And I'm going to tell her that if my name isn't on the birth certificate, I want her to allow me to legally adopt Christopher. If I have to offer her every penny I have to get her to agree to my terms, I'll do it. But he frowned as he thought about money. Margo had been acting strange about money. That first time they'd talked, she'd insinuated she wanted child support from him, but when he'd tried to pin her down about how much and how often, she'd evaded his question, saying, "Oh, we'll talk about all that later . . ."

If only this could all be resolved with money. A feeling of hopelessness crept over him. What would he do if he lost both Christopher and Ronnie? Maybe Ronnie had meant what she'd said. What if he pushed Margo, and she simply boarded a plane for Europe with Christopher?

On and on the questions raged in his mind. There seemed to be no answer to his dilemma. But there *has* to be an answer, he thought. I can't take much more of this. I'm going crazy. Even the excitement of rehearsals hadn't helped him forget his problems. Each day he'd go to the theater and wish his personal drama could be resolved as neatly and satisfactorily as the drama on the stage.

The only two bright spots in his days had been his conversations with Ronnie and his visits with Christopher. Now one was gone. Would the other be gone soon, too?

"Daddy! Daddy!" Christopher's voice piped excitedly, and his brown eyes sparkled. "Ducks!"

Alex smiled. Keeping a firm grip on the boy's hand, he kept pace with his son's short steps until they reached the edge of the pond. "Would you like to feed them?" he asked.

"Yes! Yes!" Christopher jumped up and down while Alex bought a bag of popcorn from a park vendor. A young mother grinned at them. Her own small, blonde daughter cavorted happily around her feet. Alex grinned back. When he was with Christopher, he felt almost happy, and he would forget about everything else, at least for a few hours.

I guess you can't stay depressed all the time, he thought. As Christopher squatted on the grass and threw pieces of popcorn to the squawking ducks, Alex stood, content just to watch. Finally, Christopher stood up.

"Finished, son?" Alex said softly. A jet whined overhead, pointed in the direction of LaGuardia. Alex squinted upwards. The sky looked as blue and as clear as Ronnie's eyes. There was a dull ache in his chest. *Oh, Ronnie, I need you so much. I can't stand it without you.*

Christopher nodded and said, "Uh huh." Then he lifted his arms. "Carry me?" he asked hopefully.

Alex reached down and lifted his son into his arms. The child put his left arm around Alex's shoulders and turned his face to Alex's. "Wuv you, Daddy."

Alex's heart twisted. "Love you, too, sport." He closed his eyes tightly for a minute. Christopher needed him. In the end, it all boiled down to that. Christopher was a small, dependent child, and he needed Alex. Ronnie was a grown woman, strong and capable, and she could manage just fine without him, as she'd shown him over the past weeks.

Alex stood still, hugging his son tightly. People walked past, the ducks quacked and squawked, small children whooped and hollered in the background, but Alex stood unseeing.

If I *did* push Margo, what's the worst thing that could happen? he asked himself. She'd leave. But if she had intended to go back to Europe, she'd have done it by now. She wants something else; she's just been waiting for the right moment to spring it on me. Well, I'm not going to wait a day longer to find out what it is. I'm going to walk out of this park and over to her apartment, I'm going to open the door, and I'm going to force her to give me an answer. Today.

When Kate called and invited Ronnie for Christmas, Ronnie only hesitated a few minutes. So what if Alex were there? New York City was enormous. She wouldn't be likely to run into him. Kate didn't live in

Manhattan—she had a small apartment in Brooklyn. Why not go?

"Oh, Ronnie, please come," Kate pleaded. "We'll take in some shows, stay up all night and talk . . . just like we used to."

Ronnie thought about Christmas with her brothers. About their comfortably settled lives. "Okay," she agreed. "I'll come. I'm due some vacation, anyway."

They agreed that Ronnie would come two days before Christmas and stay until after New Year's.

"I'll take you to a party New Year's Eve," promised Kate. "A photographer friend of mine is giving it, and it's sure to be a blast. We'll have a great time." Then she laughed. "Bring some sexy clothes. Maybe we'll meet some guys."

"You're just what I need right now," Ronnie said.

"I thought you sounded a little down. What's wrong?"

Ronnie heard the genuine concern in her friend's voice. "Oh, nothing much. Just a broken heart, that's all."

"Well, if that's all!"

Ronnie laughed in spite of herself. "Oh, Kate. I feel better just talking to you. When I get there I'll tell you all about him."

"Good. Sister Kate will brew pots and pots of tea and give lots and lots of sympathy, and before you know it, you won't even remember old what's-his-name!"

Margo's eyebrows lifted. "Well, you two are back much earlier than I thought you would be!" she exclaimed. "Didn't you have fun?"

"Fun!" Christopher shouted. His cheeks were red from the cold December air, and his black hair stood up on end as he snatched his red wool cap from his head and raced toward his mother.

"I wanted to talk to you, Margo. That's why we came back early."

Her golden-brown eyes glittered. "I don't have much time," she said. "I've been invited to an opening; then we're all going on to a party."

Alex noted the shimmering dress of chocolate brown satin, so complimentary to her bright hair and creamy skin. She hadn't changed, he thought. Still flitting from place to place in a constant round of parties, openings, dinner parties, house parties, you-name-it. His resolve hardened. Christopher deserved better.

She smiled, sinking gracefully onto the white sofa. Reaching for the black lacquered cigarette box on the glass coffee table, she extracted a slim cigarette, carefully and slowly lighting it with the heavy silver lighter provided for guests. She inhaled slowly.

"I thought you quit smoking," he commented.

"I did." Her topaz eyes studied him. "Now, what was it you wanted to talk about?"

"Christopher," he said bluntly. "But I'd rather not talk in front of him."

Christopher had plopped onto the white carpet and was tugging at his boots but still hadn't managed to take them off.

"Christopher, darling. Go see Sylvia and Patty," Margo said.

Without protest, Christopher got up and ran off in the direction of the kitchen.

"Okay," she said. "Talk."

"Margo, I'm through fooling around. I want to know what your plans are. Are you going to willingly allow me to be a part of Christopher's life, or am I going to have to fight you?"

Her lips quirked up at the corners, and she took a long drag on her cigarette before answering.

"It's funny you should ask," she drawled. "Yesterday I made a decision." She paused, and fear clung to the recesses of his mind like fine cobwebs in dark corners.

She tilted her head, then said, "I'm going back to Europe next week."

Five days before Christmas a small parcel arrived in the mail. Ronnie took one look at the return address and knew the package was from Alex. She placed it on the kitchen table. It sat there for two days before she could muster up enough courage to open it.

Finally, calling herself a fool for the flicker of hope she'd couldn't extinguish, she tore the brown paper off the box and opened it.

With a gasp of pleasure she lifted the exquisitely carved ivory statuette of lovebirds sitting side by side on a jade branch. Nestled into the straw packing was a small white envelope. With trembling hands, Ronnie slit the flap and withdrew the folded sheet of paper. When she opened it, two tickets fell out. She picked up the tickets. Her heart thudded against her chest. They were tickets to *Signposts*. Orchestra seats. December 26th. Ronnie knew it was literally impossible to get tickets to Alex's new play. She'd read that opening night and every other night for months to come had been sold out for weeks. Alex's fans didn't wait for the reviewers. They'd waited long enough for a new work by Alexander Summerfield.

She looked at the note. It said:

Veronica,

Please come to the opening of my play. I sent you two tickets because I thought you might like to ask your friend, Kate. I know she lives here in the city.

Without you this opening wouldn't have been possible. You were a part of the struggle to get *Signposts* into shape—you should share in the excitement of opening night.

I hope you like the lovebirds. Merry Christmas, and I'll look forward to seeing you December 26th.

Alex

Ronnie stared at the note and the tickets. Why had he sent them? The only reason she could think of was that he wanted to let her see for herself the way things were with him and Margo and Christopher. Because Ronnie knew if he really loved her, if he'd been able to work anything out, he'd have come to Juliette to see her.

But those lovebirds. Was that symbolic of something? Pain knifed its way through her as she thought of seeing Alex again . . . an Alex surrounded by admiring fans . . . and someone else. Someone with red hair and tawny eyes.

She should just throw the tickets into the wastebasket and forget the whole stupid idea. She couldn't go. She couldn't put herself through that agony.

But she tucked the tickets into her purse. She didn't have to make any decision now. Tomorrow she'd leave for Kate's, and then she'd still have three days before she had to decide whether she'd go to the opening or not.

But in her heart she knew she'd go. No matter how much it would hurt, no matter how many tears she'd shed afterward, she simply had to see Alex again.

The air vibrated with expectation and the hum of voices taut with excitement. The hum of the audience filtered through the heavy curtains. Stagehands whispered frantic last-minute instructions. Roustabouts scurried back and forth—adjusting the scrim, checking the props, marking items off on their clipboards. Jenny Campbell, the leading lady, stood in the wings in front of Alex. Her eyes were closed, and she took deep, measured breaths, exhaling through her mouth. Organized pandemonium, Alex thought. Tension fueled each person's movements.

Alex's own stomach felt as if people were racing around in it. But his nervousness wasn't entirely due to opening night jitters. No. He'd been in this state of agitation for six days now. Ever since he'd sent Ronnie the tickets.

Would she come? She *had* to be there. He'd thought about writing to her—a real letter—not that brief note he'd sent, but then he knew he couldn't tell her what he had to say in a letter. He had to see her face. He had to make her understand. And there hadn't been enough time to go to Juliette because of the opening and Christmas.

"Alex?"

Alex turned his head. Matt Oliver, the director, gave him a quizzical look. Alex grinned. "I was daydreaming."

"Curtain's going up in three minutes," Matt said.

Pent-up energy crackled around them. Suddenly, stillness settled over the people backstage. The stage area cleared, and the lights were dimmed.

Alex took a deep breath as the pulleys began to lift the trembling curtain, exposing the sea of expectant faces.

Ronnie held her breath as the curtain lifted, revealing the dimly lit set. The spotlights went up, the floodlights were turned on, and Jenny Campbell walked lightly onto the stage.

The audience clapped, and Ronnie's heart pumped harder. Oh, she hoped this play was a hit for Alex. He deserved it. She didn't allow herself to think any further, and soon, despite her inner torment, the enchantment and power of the story enfolded her.

The first act was wonderful. Ronnie had forgotten how amusing some of the scenes were, even though the subject was serious. The relationship between Elaine, played by Jenny Campbell, and Jack, played by Oscar Holland, a magnificent actor, reminded

Ronnie of her own relationship with Alex during those first weeks he'd been in Juliette.

As the curtain fell on Act I, the applause was deafening. All around her, Ronnie could feel the approval of the audience, and a bittersweet happiness gripped her. She shook her head when Kate asked her if she wanted to walk out to the lobby before Act II started.

In Act II, when Jack begins to draw away from Elaine, lured by the tempting Maria and everything that comes with her, Ronnie felt Elaine's pain. Tears threatened to spill over as Elaine bravely pretended not to care that Jack preferred flash over substance. In many ways, the story seemed to parallel Ronnie's own life.

At the next intermission, she sighed and turned to Kate. "Want to go out to the lobby and get a glass of wine or something?"

Kate grinned. "You a mind reader?"

The two women stood, merging with the crowd as they slowly made their way out to the lobby. Standing off to one side of the crowded area with glasses of wine, they observed the crowd.

"I love watching people," Kate commented. "All shapes and sizes. Aren't they something?" She chuckled. "Look at that one over there!" She pointed to a young man dressed in silver pants and vest, combined with a white chiffon shirt and high white boots. He wore a large diamond stud in his right ear.

Ronnie smiled, but her eyes restlessly searched the crowd. She wanted to see Alex. She didn't want to see Alex. Then her stomach lurched at the sight of dark hair threaded with silver. But when the man turned, he wasn't Alex. She took a sip of her wine. Her stomach felt like a whole football team was scrimmaging inside.

All around her she heard the hearty laughter and bright chattering of a crowd enjoying themselves. "The play's going to be a hit," she said.

"Yes. Old what's-his-name is talented, I'll give him that," Kate said wryly. Then she muttered under her breath, "But he's also damn stupid."

Ronnie squeezed Kate's arm and said, "Let's go back in. I don't want to miss any of the third act."

Settled back into their fourth row aisle seats, Ronnie soon lost herself in the story. The third act was the most crucial, she knew. Alex had explained about the slow build-up that takes place all through the first two acts and how in Act III the story reaches its crisis point.

"This is the most important part of the play, Ronnie," he'd said. "If I make a wrong move, I could lose the audience here. And if they're disappointed here, then it doesn't matter how good the story has been up to now."

And now Ronnie understood exactly what he'd meant. She held her breath as Maria craftily threw tidbits and Jack took them. She ached as she watched Elaine suffer but never let on to Jack that she was suffering. Ronnie gripped her hands tightly in her lap. Yes. Elaine was right. Who wanted a man because he pitied you? A woman with any guts wanted a strong man, someone who recognized her worth and was willing to fight for it.

When Jack finally saw the truth, finally understood that Maria was glitter and Elaine was gold, Ronnie's own heart beat just as fast as Elaine's, and the tears rolled down her face. She jumped to her feet with the rest of the audience and clapped until her hands hurt. The actors took curtain call after curtain call, and then the messengers flooded the center aisle, and Ronnie watched as dozens of bouquets of flowers were offered to the actors.

One of the messengers, a skinny kid of about eighteen, squatted on the floor next to their aisle and said to Kate, "You Veronica Valetti?"

Kate shook her head and pointed to Ronnie. Ronnie frowned in bewilderment as she accepted the enormous bouquet of sweetheart roses. The people sitting around them turned and looked at her. A few murmured, but in the confusion and bustle surrounding them, they soon lost interest.

A card was attached to the fragrant flowers, and with trembling fingers, Ronnie opened it. There was only one line. It said: Please come backstage for a glass of champagne when the crowd clears out/Alex. Heat flooded Ronnie's body. Her heart pounded madly.

"Well?" asked Kate.

Wordlessly, Ronnie handed her the card.

Kate whistled.

Around them, people stood up. The actors had left the stage, all the lights had gone up, and the crowd slowly emptied into the aisles.

Ronnie stood.

"Where are you going?" Kate asked.

"It's over, Kate," Ronnie said. She felt like stone.

"Sit down," Kate ordered. "We'll never be able to get backstage until these people clear out."

"I have no intention of going backstage," Ronnie said. She couldn't face him. She'd thought she could, but now she knew she couldn't stand seeing him with Margo. She wanted to be as strong as Elaine had been in the play, but she wasn't.

"Don't be ridiculous. Of course you're going."

Ronnie bit her lip and shook her head.

"Sit down!" Kate hissed. She grabbed Ronnie's arm and yanked her back into her seat.

"I don't care what you say, Kate. I've made up my mind." There was a lump in her throat that refused to dissolve.

"Okay," Kate said with a loud sigh. "If that's the way you want it. It's funny, though . . ."

Ronnie stared straight ahead.

". . . I never thought you were a coward. . . ."

Tears misted Ronnie's eyes. The lump grew bigger.

". . . I thought you were brave, strong. I thought you had guts. . . ."

Ronnie buried her face in the sweet-smelling flowers. Oh, Alex, her heart cried. I can't stand this. I can't. I want to go home.

". . . But if you want to tuck tail and run . . ."

"Damn you, Kate," Ronnie said. She swallowed, blinked, raised her head. "All right. You win. I'll go."

"Atta girl."

Ronnie turned to look at her friend and saw the satisfied smile on Kate's face. Her green eyes glittered.

Ronnie's heart lodged somewhere in the vicinity of

her throat as she and Kate climbed up to the stage area and parted the curtains.

Laughing, noisy people jammed the stage. Bottles of champagne frothed, and glasses clinked, and everyone seemed to be talking at once. Ronnie blinked, and Kate squeezed her shoulder.

"Veronica!"

The whole world stopped. Sound receded. Faces blurred. Alex stood directly in front of them. Oh, God, he's handsome, Ronnie thought. He looked wonderful in his black tux, his face flushed with success, his eyes shining as he slowly smiled. Warmth flooded his silvery eyes. Love filled her heart as she drank in each remembered feature.

Alex knew he should say something, but all he could do was stand there and look at her. She looked enchanting in a royal blue velvet dress trimmed in lace . . . like an old-fashioned painting . . . or valentine. Her huge eyes looked brilliantly blue tonight, seeming even larger than he remembered. But she looked so pale and so solemn. He wished he had the right to gather her in his arms, to kiss her the way he wanted to, to tell her how much he loved her. But he couldn't. Not yet. Maybe not ever.

He cleared his throat. "I'm so glad you came tonight."

"I am, too," she said softly. He had to strain to hear her over the noise of the others. "I'd like you to meet my friend, Kate Chamberlin."

Alex looked at her companion—a tall, slender blonde with dark green eyes. The blonde smiled faintly and extended her hand.

"Alex Summerfield," he said.

"Your play was wonderful," she said. "I was enthralled."

"Yes, Alex. The play was superb. Better even than I'd imagined it would be," Ronnie said. She smiled, but Alex saw the hint of sadness around her mouth and in her eyes.

Oh, Ronnie, he thought. Have I done this to you? I never meant to hurt you. "You deserve as much credit as I do," he said quickly.

He saw the faint pink steal into her cheeks.

"Well, well, well," boomed a hearty voice. "If it isn't the pretty little sheriff!" Bernie Maxwell's dark eyes gleamed.

Ronnie chuckled, glad to see him, glad for the interruption. She wasn't sure she could hold up much longer. She introduced him to Kate and watched as he gave her lovely friend a quick once-over.

"Are all your friends this good-looking?" he asked.

"Hey," Kate said with a smile. "I like this guy. He's got good taste."

"I'm also rich and unattached," he said. "You interested?"

Kate grinned. "You never know."

While the light banter continued, Ronnie stole a look at Alex. His eyes had never left her face, and the look he gave her made her insides roll like pitching waves in a stormy sea. He leaned close to her, and his warm breath on her neck sent a tremor through her body. "You look so beautiful tonight," he said. He touched her arm, and her heart pulsed wildly. "Let's go get you a glass of champagne."

"Kate . . ."

"Forget Kate," he said. "Bernie'll take care of her." He tapped Bernie on his arm, then cupped his hand and said something into Bernie's ear. Bernie looked up, and his dark eyes caught Ronnie's for a moment, then he nodded, and Alex said, "Thanks."

"Come on," he said to Ronnie. He grabbed her hand and pulled her along behind him. After finding her a glass of champagne, he once again clasped her free hand and led her off into the wings.

"Wait," she protested. "Where are we going?"

"You'll see," he said.

Soon Ronnie found herself following him down a flight of metal steps and into the understage area, a warren of hallways and rooms, full of people coming and going. He stopped in front of a door, knocked once, then opened it.

"Louisa," he said, "this is Miss Valetti, a friend of mine." A tall, large-boned young woman rose from a rocking chair in the corner of the dressing room. She had a small boy in her arms, a boy with jet hair and chubby cheeks. When the child turned, Ronnie saw the cleft chin, and her heart lurched. He was so beautiful. He looked exactly like Alex. The child smiled, and Ronnie felt as if someone were squeezing her heart.

"Christopher," Alex said, "this is Ronnie."

Christopher ducked his head shyly.

"Oh, Alex," Ronnie said. "He's beautiful."

"Louisa, get him ready to go home, would you? Miss Valetti and I will go with you and see him settled in."

"B . . . but . . . Kate . . ." Ronnie sputtered, her heart dancing madly. "I . . . I can't just leave . . ."

"Bernie's going to take Kate on to 21. I told him we'd be there later. That's where the party's going to be," Alex said.

Ronnie felt dazed. She drained her champagne glass and allowed Alex to help her on with her coat. Together with Louisa and Christopher, they left by the back door and walked out onto Broadway. Cars whizzed by, and fat snowflakes floated down to melt on the sidewalk.

Alex flagged a cab, and within minutes Ronnie found herself snugly enclosed next to Alex and Christopher. The child squealed with delight as Alex bounced him on his knee. Louisa sat up front with the driver, and it seemed no time at all when the cab swerved to a stop in front of an imposing building near Central Park.

Once inside Alex's apartment, Ronnie couldn't believe how fast everything had happened since the moment she'd stepped backstage. She'd never intended to be here, in Alex's home, but here she was. There was no sign of Margo.

Her traitorous heart refused to stop jumping around, and she took a deep breath to try to calm herself. She wet her lips and looked around. The apartment was furnished in an eclectic mix of contemporary and antique furniture, reflecting Alex's diverse tastes.

Louisa took Christopher and disappeared through a doorway.

"Now," Alex said. He moved close to her and took both of her hands in his. The remembered touch of his hands dissolved the last shred of calm Ronnie had managed to salvage. Her knees felt like butter, and her insides felt like the bubbles from her champagne were still at work. "Now we can talk. Something very important has happened, Ronnie, and I simply couldn't tell you about it in a letter. I had to tell you to your face."

TWELVE

This was it, Ronnie knew. If only she could be strong now. If only she could get through the next few minutes, she knew she'd be able to get through anything.

"But first," Alex continued, "let's get Christopher to bed. Then we won't have any disturbances."

Ronnie's stomach muscles unclenched at the reprieve. She quietly allowed Alex to take her hand and lead her out of the living room and down a long hallway to the other end of the apartment. He opened the last door.

Louisa was buttoning the last button on a pair of flannel pajamas, and Christopher twisted out of her hands impatiently.

"Daddy! Wonnie!" His pink cheeks glowed, and the toasty eyes were wide as Ronnie and Alex walked toward him. Alex reached for him, but Christopher, with a sly grin, said, "No! Wonnie." He held out his chubby arms, and Ronnie, as if she were someone else, reached for him. Louisa quietly left the room, closing the door behind her.

Christopher snuggled his smooth, warm cheek against hers. Ronnie loved children. But she'd never had the feeling she experienced at that precise moment. She hugged Alex's son close, breathed in the warm baby smell, and her heart hurt with an intensity that shocked her.

She knew why Alex hadn't been able to leave New York. How could he? If this were her child, she'd hang on to him with every fiber of her being . . . do whatever it took to keep him close . . . always.

Alex watched as the woman he loved held the child he loved . . . watched as her bright eyes filled with tenderness . . . watched as she stroked Christopher's dark hair. His heart swelled. He knew he was standing there like a fatuous fool, but he couldn't help himself. The sight of his son's tousled black hair next to Ronnie's dark brown curls was more beautiful than the most precious gems in Tiffany's windows.

After what seemed like hours, Alex stirred and said huskily, "Time for bed, sport."

"No!" Christopher pouted.

"I see he has a mind of his own," Ronnie said. She wished she didn't have to relinquish the child. He felt right in her arms.

"Just like his father," Alex said. Then he chuckled. "He's no fool. He knows a gorgeous girl when he sees one." His eyes softened.

Ronnie looked down. How could he tease her like this? Didn't he know how much pain she was feeling?

After a few moments they managed to extract Christopher's strong arms from their tight grip, and together they put the boy into his crib. He protested for a while, but they finally got him settled, and Alex leaned down to kiss him. Then Alex turned. "Now we can talk," he said.

He lightly touched her shoulder, his gray eyes tender. "Let's go into my office."

Ronnie walked like a sleepwalker beside him ... down the hall ... through another closed door ... into a generous-sized square room lined with bookshelves. On one side was a large brick fireplace, but the room was dominated by a huge oak desk littered with papers and pencils.

Alex shut the door and guided her to a small leather loveseat. Ronnie shivered as her skin felt the cool leather.

"You're cold," he said. "We need heat."

"Oh, no," she protested as he moved toward the fireplace. "Don't go to all that trouble."

He grinned, and her heart caught. She loved his smile. She loved him. "It's no trouble," he said. "The fireplace is fake. It's just a gas fire." He turned a lever, and merry flames leapt from the jets.

Ronnie's throat felt tight as he walked back to her, carefully moved the folds of her dress aside and sat next to her. He put his arm behind her, on the back of the sofa. But she could feel his warm flank next to her, and she held her breath as her stupid heart pounded.

Alex watched as a little pulse beat in her throat and her lower lip trembled almost imperceptibly. All his resolutions to tell her everything first suddenly evaporated, and he couldn't stand being so close without kissing her. His arm moved to her shoulders, his head lowered, and he closed his eyes.

Ronnie's heart thundered in her ears, and although her head said, "No! No!" her body refused to obey the command. Her lips parted, she lifted her head, and Alex's warm mouth covered hers.

The kiss filled her universe. Heat exploded in her body, and Ronnie allowed the heat to sweep her into its fiery center. The world tilted, and Ronnie's only coherent thought spun dizzily in her mind. Alex, Alex, Alex. She greedily clung to him, her tongue meeting his in a hunger that might never be sated.

"Oh, God, I've missed you," he groaned against her open mouth. "The taste of you, the feel of you . . ." His free hand rested on her collarbone, then moved to touch her breasts.

A shower of sensation rocketed through her. Unbearable longing consumed her. A piercing ache pulsed in her very core. Insistent. Demanding to be assuaged. Her breath came in ragged spurts. No, no, her mind screamed.

Shaking her head, she pushed at his hands, pushed at him. "Stop," she said. "Stop this." She jumped up, backed away from him.

Alex stared at her. With his flushed face and a lock of hair falling into his eyes, he reminded her of a bewildered little boy. Then she looked at his body. No. This was no little boy. This was a grown man who obviously desired her. But physical lovemaking wasn't enough anymore, she thought sadly. She needed more, and he couldn't offer more.

Suddenly she felt very calm. Her heart slowed, and she breathed evenly. "Please take me to the party, Alex," she said. "I can't do this anymore."

He stood up, smoothed his hair, drew in a shaky breath. "I'm sorry, Ronnie. I lost control of myself. I didn't mean to do that. I meant to talk to you first." He smiled wryly. "You're just too damn irresistible, that's all."

"There's really nothing to talk about, Alex. I understand . . . now that I've seen Christopher." Why drag out the agony?

Alex frowned. "Understand what?"

"Why you're committed to him. Why you can't leave him. And it's all right. I'd do the same thing if I were you."

"But that's just it! I don't have to leave him!"

Ronnie clenched her fists. She looked away from his glowing eyes. "That's nice," she said softly. "I'm happy for you." So he and his ex-wife had come to an agreement. What was it to be? A sophisticated open marriage—one where Margo would be free to indulge in her little side romances and Alex would be free to . . . Her mind refused to finish the thought. She straightened her shoulders and lifted her chin.

She met Alex's eyes, and what she saw there bewildered her. A look of love so profound it communicated itself through those calm gray eyes wrapped her in its warmth. Confusion eddied in her.

"Ronnie, darling. Don't you understand? Margo

has gone back to Europe, and she's left Christopher with me!"

Ronnie opened her mouth, but words had deserted her. She swayed, and Alex reached for her. He held her shoulders firmly. His eyes locked with hers.

"I love you, Veronica, darling," he said slowly. "I love you more than I ever thought I could love anyone. You are just as precious to me as Christopher, and until a few days ago I was afraid I'd never be able to tell you how I felt."

Joy jolted through her. "Wh . . . what about Margo?" she stammered.

Alex's hands tightened. "I don't love Margo, you dunce. I love you." Then he pulled her tight against him. She could feel his heart beating. "I love you, and I want you to marry me."

Ronnie's heart skittered, and a glorious feeling of rightness filled her as his warm mouth found hers again. This time the kiss was sweet and intoxicating. He loved her! He'd finally said it, and the words were even more beautiful, even more wonderful than she'd ever imagined they could be.

"Whew," he said softly as he dragged his mouth away from hers. "What you do to me!"

She laughed shakily. Questions whirled in Ronnie's mind. "Please, Alex," she said. "Please tell me everything."

"Margo's getting married again," he said with a grin. "Isn't it wonderful?"

"Getting married again?" Ronnie echoed.

Alex stroked her face. "Yes. She's marrying Count

Rudolph von Hagen, a very rich, very possessive Dane who has no interest in a ready-made family."

"Alex, I've got to sit down again," Ronnie said.

Together they walked to the loveseat and sat side by side, Alex's hand gripping hers tightly.

"It's really immaterial to me whether Margo marries again," he said. "All I care about is that she decided she couldn't provide the kind of home Christopher needs."

Ronnie squeezed his hand. How wonderful for him.

"I was blown away when she told me. I had marched over to her place all prepared to do battle to keep Christopher in New York with me, and all my well-rehearsed arguments were tossed out the window when she coolly informed me how she felt and what she wanted."

"But why did she wait so long to tell you?"

"She explained that. She said she wasn't sure if I'd want to be saddled with a child. She thought maybe I'd be enjoying my freedom too much, maybe I wouldn't love Christopher."

Not love Christopher! Ronnie couldn't believe it.

"I told you Margo never really knew me, Ronnie, but you didn't believe me. Anyway, she said for the first time in her life she was trying to do the unselfish thing. She said she'd always want the right to come here to visit him, and maybe when he was older, if I'd give him permission, he could go to Europe for short vacations and stay with her."

Ronnie smiled. Alex sounded so happy.

"Now, my sweet," he said. "Will you please put

me out of my misery and answer my question?" He put his hand under her chin and lifted it, gazing into her eyes. A small smile lifted the corners of his mouth.

"Oh, Alex. I love you. I've loved you from the very beginning, and I wish with all my heart I could marry you, but you know it would never work out!" Pain twisted at her insides as she said the words—but they had to be said.

"Why not?" he said incredulously. "If we love each other, why not? Is it Christopher? Don't you like the idea of my having a child, is that it?"

"Oh, don't be crazy! I fell in love with Christopher almost as fast as I fell in love with you. Couldn't you see that?" She smiled at the thought of the chubby boy and his warm baby smell.

The brilliance of Ronnie's smile dazzled Alex. My God, he thought. How had he ever found anyone as special as Ronnie? "I'm the luckiest man in the world to have found you," he said. "Now what's all this nonsense about then if it's not about Christopher?"

"Oh, God, Alex, don't you see? No matter how much I love you, I can't just walk away from my obligations. I owe something to the people of Juliette, especially people like Laurie Jacobsen and Sam."

"Who's asking you to?" Alex said.

"B . . . but . . ."

"I asked you to marry me, you nitwit, not to give up your life for me." He chucked her under her chin and kissed her lightly. His breath was warm and sweet.

Ronnie's heart skipped. "I . . . I don't understand."

"It's very simple. Even a small-town girl like you should be able to figure it all out. First, the boy says, 'I love you.' Then the girl says, 'I love you.' Then the boy and the girl get married, move to Juliette with Christopher and live happily ever after." He chuckled. "Just like any good playwright would write the script."

Ronnie sat unmoving, hardly breathing. Move to Juliette? Had she heard him right?

"So what's wrong with my scenario?" he asked.

"I couldn't ask you to move to Juliette."

"You didn't ask me. I decided all by myself."

"But, Alex," she protested. "If you do that for me, you'll eventually resent me. I don't want to have to worry about that happening the rest of my life."

"I'm not doing it for you, silly girl. I'm doing it for myself. I love Juliette. I've missed the town and all the wonderful people in it ever since I got back here. I don't have to live in the city. I can write anywhere. And when I absolutely have to come down here, we'll come together. We'll have second and third and fourth honeymoons.

"Juliette will be a wonderful place to raise Christopher and all the rest of the children we're going to have." Then he stopped, opened his eyes wide. "You *will* take time off to have children, won't you?"

A slow smile spread over her face. Happiness filled her heart. "I love you, Alex," she whispered.

"But will you marry me, madam?" he said. "Or shall I kneel?" He scrambled to his feet and dropped to one knee in front of her. He took her hands in his.

"Will you do me the honor of becoming my wife, sheriff, darling?"

"Yes, Mr. Summerfield," she said. "Yes, you fool."

"Good," he said. "Then I can give you this." Jumping up, he quickly walked to the desk, opened the middle drawer, and withdrew a small box.

As Ronnie snapped open the lid of the velvet box and saw the enormous sapphire surrounded by diamonds, she knew she must be in heaven. No other place could feel this wonderful.

Alex removed the ring and slipped it on her finger. "Perfect," he pronounced. "Matches those eyes of yours." Then he grinned. "And now, my sweet, before we go to that party, I'm going to make mad, passionate love to you. I'm going to love you so thoroughly you'll beg for mercy!"

And with that promise echoing through her heart, Ronnie surrendered to his demanding lips, lifting her arms to hold him close. This is where I belong, she thought. This is where I'll always belong.

SHARE THE FUN . . .
SHARE YOUR NEW-FOUND TREASURE!!

You don't want to let your new books out of your sight? That's okay. Your friends can get their own. Order below.

No. 5 A LITTLE INCONVENIENCE by Judy Christenberry
Never one to give up easily, Liz overcomes every obstacle Jason throws in her path and loses her heart in the process.

No. 6 CHANGE OF PACE by Sharon Brondos
Police Chief Sam Cassidy was everyone's protector but could he protect himself from the green-eyed temptress?

No. 7 SILENT ENCHANTMENT by Lacey Dancer
She was elusive and she was beautiful. Was she real? She was Alex's true-to-life fairy-tale princess.

No. 8 STORM WARNING by Kathryn Brocato
The tempest on the outside was mild compared to the raging passion of Valerie and Devon—and there was no warning!

No. 17 OPENING ACT by Ann Patrick
The summer really heats up when big city playwright meets small town sheriff.

No. 18 RAINBOW WISHES by Jacqueline Case
Mason is looking for more from life. Evie may be his pot of gold!

No. 19 SUNDAY DRIVER by Valerie Kane
Carrie breaks through all Cam's defenses and shows him how to love.

No. 20 CHEATED HEARTS by Karen Lawton Barrett
T.C. and Lucas find their way back into each other's hearts.

Kismet Romances
Dept 1190, P. O. Box 41820, Philadelphia, PA 19101-9828

Please send the books I've indicated below. Check or money order only—no cash, stamps or C.O.D.'s (PA residents, add 6% sales tax). I am enclosing $2.75 plus 75¢ handling fee for *each* book ordered.
Total Amount Enclosed: $_____.

____ No. 5   ____ No. 7   ____ No. 17   ____ No. 19
____ No. 6   ____ No. 8   ____ No. 18   ____ No. 20

Please Print:
Name_____
Address_____Apt. No._____
City/State_____Zip_____

Allow four to six weeks for delivery. Quantities limited.

Kismet Romances has for sale a Mini Handi Light to help you when reading in bed, reading maps in the car or for emergencies where light is needed. Features an on/off switch; lightweight plastic housing and strong-hold clamp that attaches easily to books, car visor, shirt pocket etc. 11" long. Requires 2 "AA" batteries (not included). If you would like to order, send $9.95 each to: Mini Handi Light Offer, P.O. Box 41820, Phila., PA 19101-9828. PA residents must add 6% sales tax. Please allow 8 weeks for delivery. Supplies are limited.